The Romance of Pilgrims

A Great American Love-Story

THE
ROMANCE
OF
PILGRIMS

A Great American Love-Story

Based on a Poem
by
Henry Longfellow

and Portraits by
Rembrandt and Friends

Written and Designed
By
David W. Bradford

Boston Hill Press

The Romance of Pilgrims
Copyright © 2006 by David W. Bradford
Published in the United States of America
All Rights Reserved.

First Edition, 2006

This book is an original, creative work,
and is protected by copyright law.

Boston Hill Press
P.O. Box 215583
Town & Country Post Office
Sacramento, CA 95821

Library of Congress Catalog No. 2006931294
ISBN-13: 978-0-9787992-1-2, Hardcover
ISBN-10: 0-9787992-1-6, Hardcover
ISBN-13: 978-0-9787992-0-5, Softcover
ISBN-10: 0-9787992-0-8, Softcover

Printed & Distributed by
LSI
La Vergne, TN 37086

Caption, Previous Illustration:
A Young Wife, Circa 1650,
Recreated portrait by Hals.
Adapted from a monochrome
published in 1921
by Deutsche Verlags-Anstalt.

Preface to The First Edition

This book retells a great American love-story from the earliest days of our nation. It is rewritten in modern English, and illustrated with hundreds of historic images. This is a fresh, new version, and not a reprint.

The story should be viewed as historical fiction, but with a distinct caveat: The original author, Henry Longfellow, claimed the tale was true.

The names of the lovers are those of real Mayflower Pilgrims who sailed to America in 1620. Portraits in this book may depict their friends or sympathizers.

Nevertheless, no concrete evidence of the love-story has ever emerged. No love-letters or confirmed portraits exist. A marriage did occur, but loveless unions were common. The love-story may only be a folk-tale.

Truth, though, lives as much in the human heart, as it does in a skeptical world. It is up to the reader to judge the truth of *The Romance of Pilgrims*.

David W. Bradford
Autumn 2006

Illustrator's Note

This book contains no modern, commercial photographs of art. Portraits and landscape paintings are adapted from old prints published before 1923 or from government archives.

Some images derive from glass negatives a century old; they reproduce portraits nearly four-hundred years old. Most have been digitally repainted to correct defects due to age, and to conform to the modernized text. Some revised images are composites of several historical individuals or landscapes.

All final images are designed for presentation in black-and-white. They recreate a by-gone age when monochrome produced vivid colors of the imagination.

THE ROMANCE OF PILGRIMS

TABLE OF CONTENTS

An American Poet
Henry Wadsworth Longfellow
(1807 – 1882)

Introduction

The *Romance of Pilgrims* is a modern adaptation of *The Courtship of Miles Standish,* a great American love-story. This legendary tale first captured the hearts of Americans in the distant year of 1858.

Published as a small pocket-book, this epic story became a runaway bestseller for decades. It had a major effect on American culture, shaping the nation's attitudes about romantic love well into the early twentieth-century.

The backdrop of the love-story was the founding of modern America by the Mayflower Pilgrims in 1620. The lovers were true-life Pilgrims.

A great-grandson wrote their story, setting it to epic verse. He related family legends heard as a child, and preserved forever in the human heart.

That child was Henry Wadsworth Longfellow, one of America's greatest poets. He is famous for such beloved poems as *Paul Revere's Ride* and the *Song of Hiawatha.*

However, Longfellow's love-story, *The Courtship of Miles Standish,* mysteriously faded from the American memory. The original text is now surprisingly difficult to read, and has become all but forgotten.

Mayflower Pilgrims pray for God's protection.
Miles Standish, a central character of the love-story, is at right, wearing steel armor. His beloved wife, Rose, embraces him. The montage is based on a mural painted in 1843 by Robert Weir for the U.S. Capitol.

(Author & U.S. Government Printing Office)

Sensation

Nevertheless, *The Courtship of Miles Standish* was once an international sensation. It sold 25,000 copies in its first weeks in America, and 10,000 copies on its *first day* in London. (In modern terms, this is equivalent to 250,000 and 40,000 copies respectively.) The epic was reprinted half a dozen times, ceasing only at the onset of the Great Depression in the 1930's.

The tale's popularity was due in part to its unique perspective: Longfellow presented the Mayflower Pilgrims as lively, everyday people, rather than remote, god-like icons.

Indeed, in Longfellow's verse, the Pilgrims were sensitive, warm-hearted souls with a passion for life. They were noble pioneers to be sure, but also laughed, cried – and loved – just like modern Americans.

History

However, *The Courtship of Miles Standish* was also notable for its uncompromising portrayal of tragic, historical events. Longfellow's epic was no sugar-coated tale; rather, it was often grimly realistic.

The narrative began in the Spring of 1621, just after a deadly first winter for the Mayflower Pilgrims in America. Half of the settlers had perished from disease; cold and starvation threatened the survivors.

Burial Hill, Plymouth, Massachusetts

The Pilgrims had other problems, too. Contrary to sugar-coated legends, relations with the Native Americans, i.e. the Indians, were not entirely peaceful.

Many natives were friendly, but others waged blood-thirsty war. Hostile Indians often threatened the settlers without provocation.

This was deeply frightening – and frustrating. Like modern Americans, the Pilgrims had difficulty accepting the notion that distant strangers wanted to harm them for little apparent reason. This caused the Pilgrims no small amount of anxiety and dissension as the settlers debated among themselves how best to respond to the threat.

Anguish

The Courtship of Miles Standish unflinchingly examined the anguish of the Pilgrims in dealing with these matters of life and death. On the one hand, the Pilgrims wanted peace, a paradise of God. Yet, they also needed to defend themselves, and that required the unthinkable – killing other human beings.

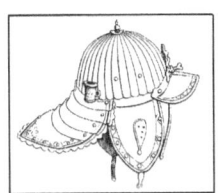

There were – and are – no easy answers. Priscilla, the heroine of the tale, speaks for us all, when she expresses horror at the battlefield ruthlessness of one her suitors. Yet, at the same time, she acknowledges the threat posed by the enemy.

That is same dilemma America faces in its modern wars. We want to be safe, but yet do not want to become that which we fight, i.e. brutal killers.

Optimism

Nevertheless, *The Courtship of Miles Standish* remains a supremely optimistic work. Its main focus, an intertwined saga of love and war, is a symbolic journey of faith for both characters and readers.

Like a Shakespearean saga, all can end well, even if we never know how or why. Simply by living life to its full, even in its most whimsical of moments, we can overcome the unrelenting shadow of death.

In this simple truth, the original author, Longfellow, was true to the religious idealism of his Pilgrim forebears. All can journey to a new, better world. All it takes is faith in the progress of a Pilgrim, one day at a time.

Faded Legend

Despite its enormous popularity in the late nine-teenth-century, *The Courtship of Miles Standish* faded from the American memory shortly thereafter. A century of global wars and economic upheavals diverted the nation from its storied past. With the sole exception of Thanksgiving, most Pilgrim legends gradually vanished from daily life.

In addition, *The Courtship of Miles Standish* had a number of technical quirks, which gradually made the tale exceptionally difficult to read. These quirks included archaic language; truncated narrative; oddly printed lines; and an awkward mimicking of Greek accents and rhythms, *a la* Homer's *Odyssey*.

A Thanksgiving Guest

Revival

This revival corrects the above defects in several ways. Shorter lines highlight the spoken cadences, while new explanatory passages and modern "free verse" emphasize clarity, rather than artificial rhythms.

Hence, this revival, *The Romance of Pilgrims*, is a new, fresh interpretation of *The Courtship of Miles Standish*. It is *not* a word-for-word reprint.

Nevertheless, the heart of the love-story remains the same. The tale begins in the Spring of 1621, six months after the arrival of the Mayflower Pilgrims in America.

A tragic epidemic has just ended. Half of the Pilgrims are dead; only fifty survivors remain. Among the mourners is Captain Miles Standish, military advisor to the Mayflower Pilgrims. His beloved wife, Rose, was among the first to die in the epidemic.

This personal loss has pushed Captain Standish to the edge of his sanity. However, he sees potential redemption in Priscilla Mullins, the only single woman still alive in Mayflower colony.

Priscilla is not only beautiful, but, to the amazement of the hardened Captain, as heroic as any soldier. Despite losing her parents in the epidemic, Priscilla nursed other sick Pilgrims at great risk to herself.

Miles Standish
In 1904, the artist, A.S. Burbank, painted this rendition of Standish and the other Pilgrim lovers (opposite page). His paintings reflect the different ages of the lovers in 1621—Standish was 37; John Alden, 22; Priscilla Mullins, 19. No actual portraits survive though; these images are only an artist's conception.
(L.C. Page & Company)

A smitten Captain Standish initiates a series of awkward events, leading to an unintended love-triangle. The soldier selects his shy housemate, John Alden, to be his agent in love. Captain Standish orders the poor fellow to carry an offer of marriage to Priscilla Mullins *on behalf of the Captain.*

The Captain is unaware that Alden is also secretly in love with Priscilla, but is too shy to do anything about it. The timid John Alden is terrified at the prospect of having to speak to the woman of *his* dreams.

Nevertheless, the unaware Captain dispatches his hapless friend to Priscilla's house. Once there, John Alden does his best to argue the Captain's case before the astonished young woman.

John Alden

The meeting does not go quite as planned. Priscilla blurts out an unexpected reply, totally disrupting the plans of her suitors. Indeed, she utters one of the most powerful one-liners in American literature.

Priscilla Mullins

Later, Priscilla adds a heart-felt defense of equality and independent womanhood. Hers is the quintessential feminist position, one that is heartwarming and moving, as it is assertive and compelling.

Regardless, the contest is on. A fierce love-triangle tests the emotional bonds of three friends, mixing love with hate, duty with desire. All of this takes place against the backdrop of a brutal Indian war, threatening the survival of the Mayflower colony.

Truth

The original source for the above tale, Henry Longfellow, always claimed that he was relating historical fact. Indeed, Longfellow accurately retells much of the famous *Mayflower* saga, albeit with poetic license. (He condensed several years of events into six months.)

Nevertheless, the love-story itself has a suspicious, Shakespearean flavor—it seems too intricate to be true.

William Shakespeare

Moreover, no hard evidence for the tale, e.g. love-letters, has ever emerged. Shakespeare, the ultimate story-teller, was still alive when the Pilgrims were young, and could easily have inspired the yarn.[1]

However, there is enough circumstantial evidence to keep the legend alive. Longfellow based his tale on oral histories that came down from the Pilgrims themselves – Longfellow was a great-grandson of the alleged lovers.

To be fair, family legends usually contain embellishments; people naturally relish telling tall-tales about their ancestors. However, in this case, something noteworthy likely occurred in reality, too.

---

[1]Shakespeare was also undergoing a popular revival in Longfellow's day.

Generations of family members were so affected, that they told and retold a highly evocative story across several centuries. Moreover, a curious fact supports the underlying truth of the romantic saga.

Golden Years

The three Pilgrims of the alleged love-triangle later moved away from Mayflower colony — together. They remained neighbors half a century into their old age.

This unusually close relationship began during their harrowing first year in America. Caught in a deadly epidemic, all three lovers made heroic efforts to save sick and dying Pilgrims during a bitterly cold winter. Like veterans of a grim war, the survivors forged a bond that endured long after their desperate battle ended.

A few years later, the three lovers established a new town, Duxbury, upon nearby Cape Gurnet, Massachusetts. Without giving away the ending of the story, the right people eventually got married.

They had many children, all eager to hear the youthful adventures of their parents.

Nobility

An affectionate ending to a stormy love-triangle is, by itself, a tale worth retelling, from generation to generation. In addition to their well-known courage, the Pilgrims are a story of unconditional love and friendship, coupled with life-long devotion and forgiveness. These are all signs of lives worth living.

These noble traits are also the essence of epic poetry, the spiritual heart of a great and kindly people. Enjoy, then, *The Romance of Pilgrims*, an adaptation of a tale by Henry Longfellow, a great-grandson of Pilgrims and Lovers.

David W. Bradford
Autumn 2006

A Reader's Guide

The Romance of Pilgrims is divided into separate acts, like that of a Shakespearean play. Each act is preceded by a scene-setting synopsis.

The text is set in large type and short lines, matching the spoken cadences. The tone is that of a breathless epic, echoing classical tales of the ancient world.

Regrettably, no portraits of the Pilgrim lovers survive. Instead, contemporary portraits of Dutch citizens, painted by Rembrandt (1606-1669) and other famed artists, serve as stand-ins for the Pilgrims.

This substitution is based on historical fact: The Mayflower Pilgrims admired the reform-minded Dutch; lived for a decade in Rembrandt's Holland; and departed for America wearing the latest Dutch fashions.

Portraits were selected from over a thousand men and women of the era. They express a romantic ideal that remains as heart-felt in our time as in theirs.

MILES STANDISH

The story begins in the Spring of 1621, six months after the arrival of the Mayflower Pilgrims in America. The settlers have established a tiny village, Plymouth Colony, on the Massachusetts seacoast.

Captain Miles Standish, their military advisor, paces about his modest cottage. He and the Pilgrims are under great stress.

A tragic winter has just ended. Half of the Pilgrims are dead from disease; only fifty survivors remain

The loss has deepened a sense of isolation. Only mysterious natives — the Indians — are nearby. Most of the natives are friendly, but some are brutally hostile.

Against this worrisome backdrop, Captain Standish and his housemate, a carpenter named John Alden, attempt to relax during a rare, idle afternoon. Their thoughts, though, soon return to recent events.

MILES STANDISH

In the days of Old Plymouth Colony,

in the land of sainted Pilgrims,

To and fro in a room

of his simple and primitive dwelling,

Strode, with a soldier's air,

Miles Standish, the Pilgrim Captain.

Buried in thought he seemed,

with hands clasped behind him,

pacing, mulling and pausing

Ever and again to behold

his glittering weapons of warfare,

Hanging in shining array

along the walls of his chamber,—

Cutlass and armor of steel,

guarding a trusty sword of Damascus,[2]

Curved at the point,

and containing,

a mystical Arabic sentence,—

While underneath, in a corner,

were a pistol,

musket, and gun-case.

---

[2]In the Middle Ages, the city of Damascus in the Middle East produced steel
swords of exceptional quality.

The Captain wore trim coat, crisp pose,

and boots of Cordovan leather.

Short of stature he was,

but strongly built and athletic,

Broad in the shoulders, and deep-chested,

with muscles and sinews of iron.

Sun-darkened was his face,

girded with red, trimmed beard,

Dusted by glimmers of snow,

the winter of life yet to come.

Near him was seated John Alden,

his friend and household companion,

Writing with diligent speed

at a table of pine by the window;

Youngest of all was Alden,

of the men who came on the *Mayflower*.

Fair-haired, azure-eyed,

with delicate Saxon complexion,

He had the glow of his youth,

and the beauty of his peoples

Whom Saint Gregory beheld,

and exclaimed,

"Not *Angles*, but Angels![3]"

———

Suddenly breaking

the silence,

and interrupting

the diligent scribe,

The Captain of Plymouth

spoke forth,

his voice prideful and boastful.——

"Look at my tools of battle," said he,

My weapons gleam in array,

Burnished so bright and clean,

as if for parade and inspection!

———

[3] *Angles* were tribal ancestors of the Pilgrims, nearly 2,000 years ago. Their name, *Angles*, derives from a Scandinavian word for "Angels."

This is the sword of Damascus;

I fought with it in Flanders;

This breastplate —

Well I remember the day!—

saved my life in a skirmish;

Here in front you can see

the very dent of the bullet

Fired point-blank at my heart

by a Spanish arcabucero[4].

Had not my armor been of sheer steel,

the forgotten bones of Miles Standish

Would now be at rest in a grave,

lost in the Flemish morasses![5]"

---

[4] An arcabucero was a soldier armed with a large gun.
[5] "Flemish morasses" refers to European battlefields of the early 1600's.

Thereupon answered John Alden,

his eyes still fixed to his writing:

"Truly the breath of the Lord

hath slackened

the speed of the bullet;

He in His mercy spared your life,

to become our shield and mighty sword!"

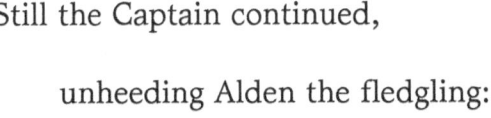

Still the Captain continued,

unheeding Alden the fledgling:

"See how brightly my weapons so gleam,

like royal jewels in a castle keep.

That is because I shined them myself,

and did not leave it to others.

Serve yourself, if you would be well served;

This is an excellent adage.

So I take care of my weapons of war

as you do, your pens and inks.

Then, too, there are my loyal troops,

    my great, invincible army,

Twelve men, all equipped,

    each with bullets and matchlock gun,

Eighteen coins a month they earn,

    together with rations and pillage,

And, like Caesar, I know the name

    of each of my mighty warriors!"

This he said with a smile,

    that sparkled in his eyes,

    glittering like sunlight

That danced on the waves of the sea,

    and then vanished in a moment.

Alden nodded, but returned to his writing,

and the Captain continued to speak:

"Look! you can see from this window

my bold gun-cannon

Planted atop our church-fortress[6],

a preacher of fire

who speaks

to the purpose,

Steady, straightforward,

and strong,

with irresistible logic,

Steadily flashing conviction

right into the heart

of the hostile.

---

[6] To economize, the Pilgrims built a single building to serve as both a chapel and as an emergency shelter.

Now we are ready, I think,

    for any offense from the Indians;

Let them come, if they like;

    the sooner they try it the better,—

Let them come, if they like,

    be it sagamore,

    sachem, or pow-wow,

Aspinet, Samoset, Corbitant,

    Squanto, or Tokamahaon![7]"

Friendly or not, I do not care;

    Only in steel and sword do I trust;

Our sacred people I shall defend!

---

[7] These are names of local Indians, mostly friendly.

Suddenly, as if exhausted

    by wars yet to be fought,

    the defender of Pilgrims fell silent.

Long at the window the Captain stood,

    and wistfully gazed upon land and sea.

A cold gray mist drifted into view,

    a vapory cloak, damp and chilled,

Shrouding forest, meadow and hill,

    along with the steel-blue rim of the ocean;

All lay silent and sad,

    in the late, lengthening day.

Over the Captain's face flitted a shadow

like those on the landscape,

Gloom intermingled with light,

a soul subdued by sadness,

A pity and regret overwhelming;

Struggling, the soldier spoke again:

"Yonder there, on the hill by the sea,

lies buried Rose Standish,

My beautiful flower of love,

who perished by the wayside.

She was the first to die

of all who came

on the *Mayflower*.

Gently above her

is swaying

the field of wheat

we have sown,

Better to hide from Indian scouts

the sad graves of our beloved—

Lest the spies should count them

and see our numbers diminished!"

Sadly the Captain averted his face,

strode up and down,

and was thoughtful.

Fixed to his cottage wall

was a shelf of books;

Stood in their midst

Were three tomes prominent,

all much alike for size and shape;

Two were about man and earth,

and one about God and Heaven,

Respectively, Bariffe's Artillery Guide,

and the Commentaries of Caesar,

(the great Roman general);

And, as if guarded by these,

ruling in their midst, the Bible.

Musing and gazing upon his books,

    Miles Standish paused, as if doubtful;

Which of his books should he choose

    for his consolation and comfort?

Was it legendary wars of Hebrews,

    or famous campaigns of Romans,

Or thunderous artillery and cannon

    for serious, well-aimed Pilgrims?

Finally, down from its shelf,

    he dragged the ponderous Caesar,

Seated himself at the window,

    placed the book in his lap,

    and, in silence,

Turned over the well-worn pages;

  Soon he was lost in a world of war,

Following the marching boots,

    signaling the heat of the battle.

Nothing then was heard in the room

    but the hurrying pen of Alden the fledgling,

Busily writing epistles important,

    to go by way of the *Mayflower,*

Ready to sail on the morrow,

    if God were so willing,

Bound for England with news

    of all that terrible winter,—

Half their number dead,

    only a few families remaining.

Yet, also written by Alden,

    were mentions of the maiden Priscilla;

Nay, his letters were filled

    with the name and fame

    of the Pilgrim maiden Priscilla!

LOVE AND FRIENDSHIP

The two housemates, Captain Standish and John Alden, continue a leisurely afternoon in silence. Alden finishes writing his letters, while the good Captain reads the autobiography of Julius Caesar, the legendary general of the Roman Empire.

When both finish their diversions, their conversation begins anew. They discuss two favorite subjects for men of all eras – war and women.

However, neither man is quite prepared for what follows. They become more involved in their conversation than either expects.

LOVE AND FRIENDSHIP

Nothing was heard in the room

   but the hurrying pen of Alden the fledgling,

Or an occasional sigh of excitement

   from the pounding heart of the Captain,

Reading of the glorious battles

   of the mighty General, Julius Caesar.

After a while the Captain exclaimed,

   with a great flourish and gesture,

Sweeping across his open book:

   "A wonderful man was this Caesar!"

                You and I

                    cannot compare,

                    for we are

                    both mortal;

              You are a writer,

                    and I am a fighter,

                    but here is a fellow

              Who could both

                    write and fight,

   and in both was equally skillful!"

Straightway answered John Alden,

   fair-haired and youthful:

"Yes, Caesar was talented, as you say,

   with both pen and sword together.

Somewhere I have read,

—but where I forget—

Caesar did stroke

Seven letters at once,

while quietly writing his memoirs."

"Truly," continued the Captain,

not heeding or hearing John Alden,

"Truly a wonderful man was

General Julius Caesar!

Better be first, Caesar said,

    in a little Iberian village,

Than be second in Rome;

    and I think he was right

    just as he said it;

Better to be free

    in a far-away land,

    than to serve an imperial lord,

Better to struggle in a hard, new world,

    than to grovel in the court of the King!

So, listen here now as I tell

of wonderful Caesar

and his mighty deeds:

Twice Caesar was wed

before he was twenty,

and many times thereafter.

Five-hundred battles he fought,

and a thousand cities

he conquered;

He, too, fought in Flanders,

and wrote his memoirs clearly;

Alas, sadly he was slain,

cruelly, with treachery,

stabbed by his friend,

the once dear Brutus, a sparkling orator!

Thus ended the career

of the mighty great Roman,

General Julius Caesar;

Still, let us remember great Caesar

on a certain occasion in Flanders,

 When his rear-guard retreated,

his front gave way,

And his immortal Twelfth Legion

crowded too closely together,

unable to wield their weapons.

All were on the verge of defeat,

    but Caesar seized the moment,

        Leapt straight

          to the head of the army,

          and boldly commanded

          the captains,

        Calling each by name,

as he sounded the hue and cry of battle!

Deploying his troops,

    Caesar sharpened their aim,

    ranged their weapons,

And charged the enemy,

    capturing the field of glory!

So Caesar won the day,

    the battle of something-or-other.

That's what I always say:

    if you wish a thing to be done well,

Then you must do it yourself,

    and cannot leave it to others!"

All was silent again;

    the Captain continued his reading.

Nothing was heard in the room

    but the hurrying pen

    of Alden the fledgling,

Busily writing epistles important

    to sail the next day

    by way of the *Mayflower;*

No missive, though,

    was more important,

    than the name and fame

    of the Pilgrim maiden Priscilla;

Every sentence began or closed

    with the name of Priscilla,

Till the treacherous pen,

    which guarded the sensitive secret,

Strove to betray it by singing

    and shouting the name of Priscilla!

In a while, the Captain closed his book,

with a bang of its ponderous cover,

Sudden and loud, as if cracking

the floor with boot and musket.

Then to Alden the younger

spoke Standish, the elder:

"When you finish your writing,

let me speak a matter important;

Be, though, not in hurry or haste;

I shall not be impatient."

Straightway Alden sat erect,

as he folded

the last of his letters;

He pushed his papers aside,

and gave respectful attention:

"Speak; for whenever you speak,

I am always ready to listen,

Always ready to hear and to heed

my dear friend, Miles Standish."

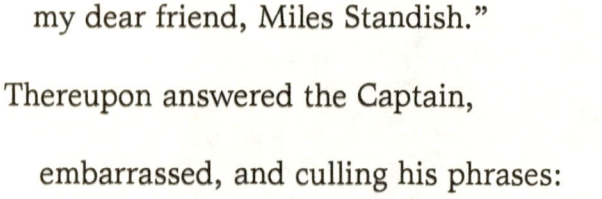

Thereupon answered the Captain,

embarrassed, and culling his phrases:

"'Tis not good for a man to be alone,

thus sayeth the Bible

and Scripture.

This I have said before;

again and again I repeat it ——

Every hour in the day,

I think it, I feel it, and I say it.

Since Rose Standish died,

   my life has been weary and dreary;

Sick at heart have I been,

   without friendship and comfort.

Hope, though, follows despair,

   God's grace delivered;

Now in my lonely hours

   come thoughts

   of the Pilgrim maiden Priscilla.

She is alone in the world;

her father, mother, and brother

Died in the winter together;

I saw her coming and going,

Day-by-day, mourning the somber graves,

while still bravely nursing her neighbors.

She being so patient, courageous, and strong,

then and there, I knew,

That if angels walked the earth,

    as angels dwell in heaven,

Then two have I seen and known;

    One is gone, but the other is Priscilla.——

She comes to fill the emptiness

    which the other sadly abandoned.

Long have I cherished Priscilla

but never dared to admit it,

Being a coward in this,

just as I am

valiant in battle.

Go hence to damsel Priscilla,

the loveliest maiden

of Plymouth,

And say that a blunt old Captain,

skilled in action, not speech,

Offers his hand and heart in marriage,

a life with a warm-blooded soldier.

Say it, though, not with my words,

but something akin to my meaning;

This you must do,

I cannot do it myself;

I am a maker of war,

and not of delicate phrases.

You, who are bred as a scholar,

    can say it in elegant language,

Singing in soft, delicate whispers

    about the doings and wooings of lovers,

So gracefully as best can be assured

    to win the heart of a maiden."

After the Captain spoke, John Alden,

　　the fair-haired, sensitive fledgling,

Was aghast at the disclosure,

　　surprised, embarrassed, and bewildered,

Trying to mask his dismay

　　by treating the subject with lightness,

Trying to smile and be calm

　　when his heart was struck by lightning.

Alden then chattered and spoke,

    much more stammering than answering:

"Such a message as that,

    I fear I would mangle and mar;

If you would have it done well,—

    I am only repeating your proverb,—

Then you must do it yourself;

    You must not leave it to others!"

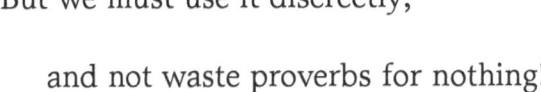

But with the air of a soldier

    intent on his purpose,

And gravely shaking his head,

    Captain Standish firmly retorted:

"Truly my proverb is good,

    and I cannot rightly deny it;

But we must use it discreetly,

    and not waste proverbs for nothing!

Now, as I said before,

    I was never a maker of phrases.

I can march up to a fortress

    and summon the place to surrender,

But march up to a woman

    to ask for her hand, I dare not.

I'm not afraid of bullets,

    nor that from the mouth of a cannon,

But a thundering 'No!' point-blank

    from the mouth of a woman,——

That I confess gives me terror,—

    nor am I ashamed to confess it!

So you must grant my request,

    for you are an elegant scholar,

Having the grace of speech,

    and can turn a flattering phrase."

———

Grasping the hand of John Alden,

    who was still reluctant and doubtful,

The Captain held it to beg,

    and added

    ever so softly:

"Though I have thus far

    spoken calmly,

    yet deep is the feeling

    that prompts me;

Surely you can not refuse me;

    I ask it in the name of our friendship!"

Then made answer John Alden:

"The bonds of friendship are sacred;

What you demand in its name,

I cannot rightly deny you!"

So the strong-willed Captain prevailed,

turning aside youth and gentility;

Alas, friendship prevailed over secret love,

and boy Alden went on his errand.

THE LOVER'S ERRAND

John Alden departs reluctantly for Priscilla's house, leaving Captain Standish alone in his cottage. The good Captain, despite contemplating sacred love and marriage, calmly goes back to reading about the arcane wars of Julius Caesar.

Like any confident commander, Captain Standish believes he has firmly delegated his objective to a trusted lieutenant, John Alden. The latter vows earnestly to win the Pilgrim maiden for the good Captain; Alden sadly plans to end his own secret love for her.

However, Priscilla Mullins proves to be a very independent-minded woman. Upon hearing John Alden's proffer of marriage on behalf of Captain Standish, she utters an unforgettable reply. In the blink of an eye, the courtship of Miles Standish goes awry.

THE LOVER'S ERRAND

So the strong-willed Captain prevailed,

    and Alden went on his errand,

Through the streets of the village,

    and into the paths of the forest;

All about Alden was life,

    the Great Spirit revealed.——

Bluebirds and robins fluttered

    amidst the tranquil woods,

Singing from nests of sky and tree;

    They nursed their fledgling, sweet young,

While praising peaceful, aerial cities

    of joy, affection, and freedom.

Yet, a troubled man sees not

    the joy of this world;

All around Alden was peace,

    but within him, passions contended —

Love with desire, duty with need —

    burdening every generous impulse.

Alden felt like a foundering ship,

    shaken by the roll of the vessel;

He was lashed by a bitter sea,

    and the merciless surge of the ocean.

To and fro in his breast

    his thoughts were heaving and hewing.

"Must I relinquish her so,"

    he murmured painfully,

"Must I relinquish her so,

    the joy, the hope, and the illusion?

Was it for this I loved,

    waited, and worshiped

    in silence?

Was it for this

    I tempted death

Over the wintry sea,

    to the desolate shores

    of New England?

———

Or was it all self-deception,

    a fantasy of my own making?

Oh! Truly the heart is deceitful!

    And out of its depths are corruption;

Much rises in exultation,

with misty phantoms of passion;

Angels of light they seem,

but are really delusions of Satan.

All is clear to me now;

I feel and see it so clearly!

This is the hand of the Lord;

It is laid upon me in anger,

For I have followed too much

my heart's desires and devices,

Worshiping Ashtoreth blindly

along with impious idols of Baal,

Pagan gods of fools,

and fearful demons of destruction.

They are the cross I bear,

the sin and the swift retribution."

———

So through the Plymouth woods

John Alden went on his errand;

Crossing the brook at the ford,

where it bubbled through pebble and shallow.

Yet, as he went,

charmed he became,

by May-flowers

blooming around him.

Sweet was the air with their fragrance,

and the blossoms shone brightly

with their beauty,

Glowing like dear children,

asleep in the shade of the forest.

"Pilgrim flowers,"

whispered John Alden,

"fine orchids

for Pilgrim maidens,

Modest, simple, and sweet,

the very glory of Priscilla!

So I shall pick them for her,

for Priscilla, the May-flower of Plymouth.

Modest, simple, and sweet,

A parting gift they shall be;

Breathing their silent farewells,

as they fade, wither and perish,

Soon to be abandoned forever,

as is the heart of the giver."

So through the Pilgrim woods

    John Alden went on his errand;

He entered a forest clearing,

    and beheld a glimpse of the ocean,

Sail-less, somber and cold

    with lingering breath

    of damp east wind.

He soon saw people at work in a meadow,

    then came upon a new-built house;

He stepped to its door,

and heard a musical voice

Singing the hundredth Psalm,

an uplifting anthem of yore,

A sacred prayer of Luther,[8]

sung to the music of the poet,

Full of the breath of the Lord,

consoling and comforting many.

Alden knocked & peered into the open door,

beholding the form of the maiden,

Seated and spinning at her wheel[9],

surrounded by snowy drifts of wool,

Nestling gently up to her knees;

Delicately she turned a spindle,

While her foot pumped a pedal,

guiding the wheel in its motion.

----

[8] Martin Luther began the Reformation of the Christian Church in 1517.
[9] The "wheel" is a spinning-wheel, which twists wool into yarn or thread.

Open on her lap lay an aged book

   graced with the psalms of Ainsworth,[10]

Printed in Amsterdam long ago,

   the lyrics and music together,—

Rows and rows of curling notes

   sung in graceful, ancient churches,

Enlivened and brightened

   by the dancing vine of their verses.

---

[10]Henry Ainsworth was an English minister, sympathetic to the Pilgrims.

Sing did the Pilgrim maiden,

enchanting her home

and a forest cathedral,

Making them beautiful

with soft grace,

and rich with

the wealth of her being.

Over Alden came, like a wind

that is keen, cold and relentless,

Thoughts of what might have been,

adding to the weight and woe of his errand. —

All his dreams were fading

all hopes vanishing,

All life's future

a dreary and

empty mansion,

Haunted by sad regrets,

and pallid, sorrowful faces.

Still he whispered to himself,

   and almost fiercely he said it:

"Let not him that places his hand

   upon the plow

   turn from his task;

Even if the plow cut through

   the flowers of life

   to its fountains,

Even if it pass

   over the graves of the dead

   and the hearths of the living,

It is the will of the Lord;

   So shall His mercy

   endureth, forever."

Then Alden entered the house,

   suddenly ending the chorus

Of hymn, whim & spinning wheel;

   Man and moment had arrived.

Fair Priscilla rose as he entered,

extending her hand in welcome,

And said, "I knew it was you,

when I heard your steps;

For I was thinking of you,

as I sat here singing and spinning."

Alden was awkward and numb with delight;

   she had mingled thoughts of him

With work and sacred hymn,

   all from the heart of a maiden.

His love need not be lost,

   courage might yet bring hope;

Yet, silent before her he stood,

   struggling for words

   for his feelings...

—— Finally he presented his flowers,

   while thinking

   of a day last winter,

After the first great snow,

   when he beat a path

   from the village,

Reeling and plunging

   through the drifts

   that surrounded her house.

When he entered her doorway,

Priscilla had smiled,

Laughed at the snow in his hair,

offered the warmth of her hearth,

And was grateful and pleased

that he braved the tempest for her.

Had he but spoken then,

all might now be different;

Now it was all too late;

the golden moment had passed!

So he stood there abashed,

and gave her flowers for an answer.

Then they sat down and talked

of the birds and beautiful spring,

Talked of their friends in England,

and the *Mayflower's* sailing on the morrow.

"I've been thinking all day,"

    said softly the Pilgrim maiden,

"Dreaming all night, and thinking all day,

    of hedge-rows in England,—

They are in blossom now,

    and green as a garden.

I thought of

    lanes and fields,

    and songs of lark,

    and nightingale;

I could see

    the village street,

    and friendly neighbors

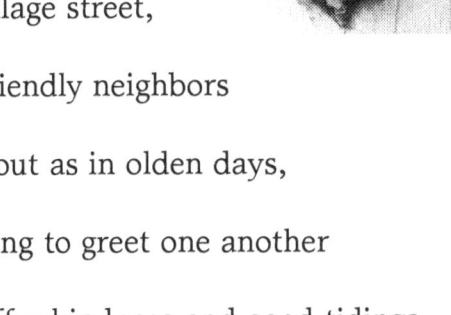

Going about as in olden days,

    stopping to greet one another

    and offer kindness and good tidings.

And, in the meadow of the village green,

    stood our ancient church,

With wondrous ivy climbing

    a simple gray tower,

honoring the weathered graves of our kin."

Sighing, the Pilgrim maiden paused,

    dreamy-eyed and gazing afar,

Silent and reflecting,

    a woman of two lands and one soul.

"Kindly and decent are the people here,"

said she, softly anew,

"and dear to me in my religion;

Still my heart is so sad,

that I wish myself

back in Old England.

You will say it is wrong,

but I can not help it;

Sometimes I do wish

I were back in Old England,

and not in a lonely new world."

Thereupon answered boy Alden:

"Nay, I do not blame you;

Many a troubled soul

have quailed

in this terrible winter.

Your heart is tender and trusting,

and needs a stronger to lean on;

So I have come to you now,

 with an offer and proffer of marriage

Made by a man good and true,

 Miles Standish, the Captain of Plymouth!"

Thus he delivered his message,

 the nimble writer of letters ——

He did not embellish the theme,

 nor arrayed it in beautiful phrases,

But came straight to the point,

and blurted it out like a schoolboy;

Even the gruff Captain himself could hardly

have said it more bluntly.

Mute with amazement and sorrow,

Priscilla, the Pilgrim maiden,

Stared into the face of boy Alden,

her eyes widened with wonder,

Feeling his words like a blow,

all but rendering her speechless,

Till at length she exclaimed,

interrupting the discomforting quiet:

"If the great Captain of Plymouth

is so very eager to wed me,

Why does he not come himself,

and take the time to woo me?

If I am not worth the wooing,

Surely I am not worth the winning!"

Then boy Alden began explaining,

seeking to smooth the matter,

But making it worse as he went,

saying the Captain was busy,

Had no time for such things...

—*such things*!

The words grated and stung,

Hurting sensitive Priscilla;

And swift as a flash

she replied:

"He hasn't time

for *such things*,

when 'No' may

yet be my answer;

Would he have the time – or make it –

after we are wed,

and my choice is not so?

That is the way with you men;

either you fail a woman's needs

or can never know or try.

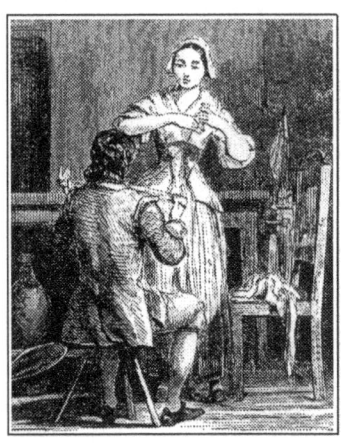

When you men make up your minds,

    after thinking of this woman or that,

Choosing, selecting, and rejecting,

    comparing one with another,

Then you make known your desire,

    with abrupt and sudden avowal,

And are offended and hurt,

    when the fair-haired maiden

Does not quickly embrace

a love she never suspected!

She cannot attain at a bound

the height of your hopes;

This is not right nor just:

For surely a woman's affection

Is not so easily had;

Love is more than just asking.

Rather, when true love rules,

only deeds, not words will do.

Had Captain Standish but waited a while,

had he sent love, not words,

Even this Captain of yours—who knows?—

might yet have won my heart,

His rough edges aside;

But now *that*

can never happen."

Yet, boy Alden went on,

unheeding the words

of Priscilla,

Urging the case of his friend,

explaining, persuading, and expanding.

John Alden spoke of the Captain,

as having courage and skill,

in his great battles in Flanders[11],

---

[11] Flanders was a medieval country in northwestern Europe.

How with the people of God

    Standish the soldier suffered and lost;

How, in return for his devotion,

    he became Captain of Pilgrims.

Nay, not lightly was he chosen,

    but with proud lineage in mind;

Miles Standish was noble born,

    tracing his pedigree plainly,

Back to Hugh Standish of Duxbury Hall,

    in medieval Lancashire, England;

Ralph the Elder was the Captain's father,

    the first son of Thurston de Standish,

Heir unto vast estates,

    of which he was basely defrauded —

Trials and tribulations

    the family always endured. —

Thus, proudly the Captain wore

    his kinsmen's coat-of-arms,

    a crested hawk of gallant silver,

Combed and woven in red,

    and placed in a great medallion.

Standish was a man of honor,

   of noble and generous nature;

Though rough at the edges,

   kindly he could be;

   All knew his winter's mission

When he attended the sick

   as gently as an angel.

Somewhat hasty and hot,

Standish could not deny it,

being headstrong and

Stern as a soldier might be;

Yet, none should scorn or dismiss him;

His temper was in quick passing,

and never too sharp.

Rather he was great of heart,

magnanimous, courtly,

and courageous;

Any woman in Plymouth,

nay, any woman in England,

Might be happy and proud

to marry gallant Captain Standish!

But as John Alden

warmed and glowed,

in his simple

and eloquent language,

Quite forgetful of self,

and full of the praise of Standish,

Slyly the maiden smiled,

   with eyes overrunning with laughter,

And said in a tremulous voice,

   "Why don't you speak

   for yourself, John?"

JOHN ALDEN

Terrified by Priscilla's discovery of his secret love for her, John Alden flees her house. However, he does not know where to go or what to do.

Alden can no longer nurture secret fantasies of love eternal. Priscilla will now either accept him or reject him, forever.

There is also the ticklish problem of Captain Standish. The burly soldier will not be pleased. His trusted lieutenant, John Alden, bungled his mission to win the Pilgrim maiden for the good Captain. Worse, Alden may be a traitor, desiring the very same woman.

Bewildered, John Alden wanders aimlessly through the countryside. Almost by accident, he finds himself at the beach, where he painfully ponders his future.

JOHN ALDEN

John Alden rushed into the open air,

like a man thoroughly insane,

Perplexed, bewildered, and lost,

wandering alone by the sea-side.

He paced up and down the sands,

　　and bared his head to the east wind,

Cooling his heated brow,

　　and the fire and fever within.

Mystical images drifted through his head,

　　of fact or fancy could not be said;

Slowly, as if out of the heavens,

　　with apocalyptical splendors

Descended the City of God,

　　into the view of Saint John, Christ's Apostle.

There, above shrouded walls

    of star-fire, jasper, and sapphire,

Sank the broad red sun,

    over towering turrets uplifted

And the shimmering gold of the angel

    who measured the city's glory.

"Welcome, O wind of the East!"

Alden exclaimed in wild exultation,

"Welcome, O wind of the East,

from the swirl of the misty Atlantic!

Blow over waves of crimson reeds,

and measureless meadows of sea-leaves,

Blow over rocky wastes,

and the grottoes and gardens of ocean!

O great God,

    lay thy cool, moist hand

    on my burning forehead,

    and hold me

Close in thy garments of mist,

    to allay the fever within me!"

~~Like an awakened conscience,

    the sea moaned and tossed in reply,

Beating remorseful and loud

    upon the shifting sands of the sea-shore.~~

Fierce in Alden's soul

    became the struggle

    of passions contending;

Love triumphant and crowned,

    — friendship wounded

    and bleeding —

Clashed with passionate cries of desire

    and relentless pleadings of duty!

 "Is it my fault," Alden asked,

"that the maiden has chosen between us?

Is it my fault the Captain has failed,—

my fault that I am the victor?"

———

Then thundered a voice within,

like that of the Prophet:

"It hath displeased the Lord!"

Then forbidden thoughts

of King David's sins[12],

Stealing Bathsheba,

the wife of another,

mingled with Alden's own guilt,

Until they became one and the same,

fusing Biblical King and devout Pilgrim;

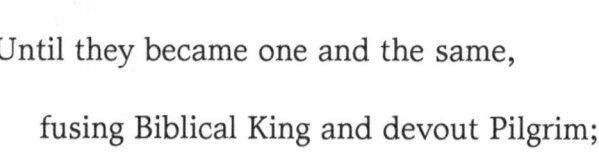

---

[12]King David was a great ruler of ancient Israel. Nevertheless, God punished him for stealing another man's wife.

King David betrayed husband and God—

Had Alden betrayed friend and same?

The question stirred and contrasted

with the ever gallant

Captain Standish,

always so noble in battle.

†††

Shame and confusion of guilt,

　　awash in fear and dreaded lament,

Overwhelmed Alden at once,

　　making him cry in deepest contrition:

"It has angered the Lord!

　　It is the temptation of Satan!"

Then uplifting his head,

　　he looked at the sea,

　　and beheld with his own eyes

Dimly a shadowy form;

　　The sacred *Mayflower* rode at anchor,

Rocked on the rising tide,

　　and ready to sail on the morrow.

Alden heard the ship speak

through the mist of the sea,

The wooden creak of her hull,

along with echoes of mates

and sailors shouting "Aye, aye!"

Clear and distinct the sounds were,

but not loud nor grating,

in the cool damp of twilight.

Alden stood still for a moment,

   listening and watching the vessel,

Then went hurriedly on,

   like a man chasing a phantom,

Stopping, then quickening his pace,

   and following the beckoning shadow.

———

"Yes, it is plain to me now," he murmured;

   "the hand of the Lord

Leads me from darkness,

   and my bondage of error.

Across this heavy sea

   I shall go;

God shall lift a watery wall behind me,

Hiding and protecting me

   from the cruel thoughts that pursue me.

Back I will go over the ocean,

    leaving this dreary land of Pilgrims,

Along with her whom I may not love,

    and him whom my guilt has offended.

Better to be in my grave

    in the old churchyard in England,

Close to my mother's side,

    and among the dust of my dear kind;

Yes! Better be dead and forgotten,

    than living in shame and dishonor!

Safe, sacred, and unseen,

  in the darkness of my narrow tomb,

With me my secret

  shall lie,

  like a buried jewel that glimmers

Bright on the dead hand of dust,

  in the chambers of silence and doom.

Yes! I shall wear the 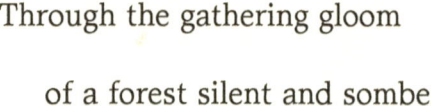 wedded ring

  of the great espousal hereafter!"

———

Thus as he spoke, forward he marched,

  in the strength

  of his strong resolution,

Leaving behind him the shore,

  and hurrying along

  in the twilight,

Through the gathering gloom

  of a forest silent and somber,

Till he beheld the lights

  of the seven houses of Plymouth,

Shining like seven stars

  through the mist of the evening.—

Alden entered a doorway

  and found the

  redoubtable

  Captain

Still reading

  and absorbed

  in the warrior saga of Caesar,

Fighting some great campaign

  in Hainaut, Brabant or Flanders[13].

"Long have you been on your errand,"

  said Standish with cheery demeanor,

Expecting without doubt a sweet reply,

  and coolly ignoring a possible retort.

---

[13] These were medieval countries in Northern Europe.

"Not far off is the house of the maiden,

    though many woods are between us;

But you have lingered so long,

    that while you were going and coming

I fought ten battles with Caesar

    and crushed and captured a city!

Come, and sit down,

and in quick order,

tell me all that has happened."

Then John Alden spoke,

and related the wondrous adventure,

From beginning to end,

just as it happened;

How he had seen Priscilla,

and courted her quickly,

How he softened her smoothly

   and politely deflected her refusal.

But when he finally came

   to tell the words of Priscilla,

Words so tender and cruel,

   "Why don't you speak for yourself, John?"

Up leapt the Captain of Plymouth,

Loudly stomping the floor,

rattling the knight's armor,

That hung loosely on the wall,

yielding a sinister, clanging omen.

The Captain's wrath burst forth

with a sudden, horrible explosion,

Much like a weapon of war,

that spreads and scatters destruction.

Wildly the Captain shouted, and harshly so:

"Betrayed me you did, John Alden!"

Me, Captain Standish, your friend!

You supplanted, defrauded, and betrayed!

My ancestors struck deeply with sword

all traitors to King and Lord;

What shall prevent me

from doing the same, to you, boy Alden?

For yours is the greater treason,

for you are a traitor to friendship!

Yes! You are a traitor to friendship,

    foul, fiendish, and despicable!

You, John Alden, who lived under my roof,

    whom I cherished and loved as a brother;

You, who sat at my table,

    and drank from my cup,

You, who sullied my honor,

    and thoughts so sacred,—

What is between us now

    after friendship so scorned?

———

Brutus was Caesar's friend,

    and you were mine,

        But traitors are one and the same;

        'You, too, Brutus!' say I.

        Ah, woe to friendship hereafter!

Nothing stands between us

    but war and implacable hatred!"

So roared the Captain of Plymouth,

    as he strode about in the chamber,

Adamant and choking with rage,

    swelling the veins of his temples.

But in the midst of his tantrum

    a man appeared at the doorway,

Bringing in quick-time haste

    a message of urgent importance —

Rumors of war,

and hostile incursions of Indians!

Straightway the Captain paused,

and, without further question or parley,

Took from the post on the wall

his sword and scabbard of steel,

Buckled its harness, fitted his helmet,

and, frowning fiercely, departed.

Alden was left alone in the cottage dark;

The rattling saber of the Captain

Could still be heard, step by step,

fading away in the distance.

Alden rose from his chair,

stepped to the open door,

And stared into the outer darkness;

A cool breeze soothed his hurt feelings.

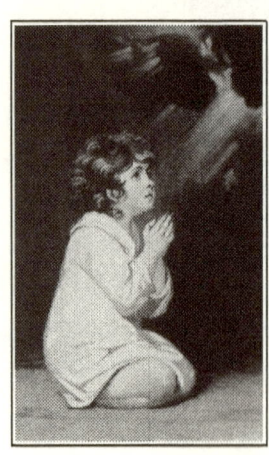

Then he lifted his eyes

to the heavens,

placed his hands

in a child-like pose,

And prayed, whispering,

in the silence of the night

to the Father who seeth in secret.

Meanwhile the inconsolable Captain

strode wrathful to the council of Plymouth,

Found it already assembled,

and impatiently awaiting his coming;

They were in the middle of life,

austere and grave in deportment,

Only one of them old,

the tallest hill, nearest to God;

His hair was snow-white, his faced lined,

   he being the excellent Elder of Plymouth,

   the venerable William Brewster.

No man could be more wise,

   no tribe better led, fine or divine——

God had sifted three kingdoms of Britain

   to find the wheat for this planting,

Then had sifted the wheat,

as the living seed of a new nation——

So say the chronicles of old,

and such is the faith of the people!

———

Near them in council,

was invited an Indian,

stern and defiant,

Naked to the waist,

grim and ferocious in aspect;

While on the table

before them

was lying solidly a Bible,

Ponderous, bound in leather,

brass-studded, printed in Holland.

Beside it glittered a stuffed skin

of rattlesnake arrayed,

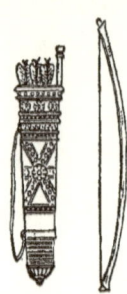

Filled, like a quiver, with arrows,

a signal and challenge to war;

The Indian brought the omen

with a sharp tongue of defiance——

Treasure and submission he demanded,

death and destruction he promised.

All this the Captain beheld,

watching wise men debating

As to the proper answer befitting

the hostile message and menace.

They talked of this and of that,

contriving, suggesting, objecting;

Only one voice sought peace,

and that was Brewster the Elder,

Arguing so wisely and well

that some were calmly swayed;

None need die or kill, he said,

for this was but Christian behavior!

Then out spoke Miles Standish,

the stalwart Captain of Plymouth,

His eyes red with fury,

    his voice choking with anger:

"No!" shouted he, "Who can make war

    with milk, honey, and roses?

Is it to shoot red squirrels

    that we have planted our cannon

High on the roof of our church,

    or is it to shoot red devils?

Truly the only word

    understood by a savage

Is the cry of fire and smoke

    from the mouth

    of a cannon!"

Thereupon answered and spoke

    the excellent Elder of Plymouth,

All but amazed and alarmed

    by the Captain's

    insult and scorn:

"War is not the way of Saint Paul,

    and all Christ's Apostles;

Not from the mouth of a cannon

    were their words of fire and truth!

Peace is our aim, love is our weapon,

    carry it through, all can be well."

————

But unheeded fell the rebuke;

    Hate seized the Captain's soul,

Urging him to the Elder's table,

    and forcefully seeking battle:

"Leave this matter to me,

    for to me by right it revolves!

War is a terrible endeavor;

    but in a cause that is righteous,

Sweet is the sound of the cannon's roar;

    and thus I answer the challenge!"

Then from the rattlesnake quiver,

    with a sudden and contemptuous gesture,

He discarded the Indian's arrows,

    and poured gunpowder and bullets,

Filling the serpent's skin

and handed it

back to the savage,

Barking, in thundering tones:

"Here, take it! This is your answer!

In an exchange, bullet for arrow,

eye for eye, tooth for tooth!"

—Silently out of the room

then glided the hostile native,

Bearing the serpent's skin,

    and harboring thoughts unthinkable,

Winding his singular way in the dark

    back to the depths of the forest.

THE SAILING OF THE MAYFLOWER

Alerted by the Indian ultimatum, Captain Standish quickly gathers volunteer soldiers from Plymouth Colony. They are joined by their faithful Indian guide, Hobomok. Conspicuously absent from the war party is John Alden.

Standish and his militia pursue the hostile Indians into the forest. The remaining Pilgrims wait anxiously for their return.

Meanwhile, the Mayflower, *the legendary ship of the Pilgrims, prepares to sail back to England without them. The ship's crew are not Pilgrims, but regular sailors, eager to return home.*

The Pilgrims gather at the beach to bid a poignant farewell: The settlers have deliberately chosen to be stranded forever in the American wilderness.

THE SAILING OF THE MAYFLOWER

In the gray light of dawn,

    as cool mists shrouded the meadows,

There was a stir and sound

    in the slumbering village of Plymouth,

The clatter and clicking of weapons,

    and the order imperative, "Forward!"

Uttered in tones suppressed,

    followed by the trample of boots.

Ten figures in the mist,

    marched slowly out of the village.

Standish the stalwart commanded,

    with eight of his valorous army,

Led by their Indian guide, brave Hobomok,

    friend of the Pilgrim peoples,

Marching inland to quell

    the sudden danger of a brutal foe.

Giants they seemed in the mist,

    or brave warriors of Hebrew King David,

Gallant soldiers of the Lord,

    who believed in God and the Bible,—

Aye, who believed in smiting

    the ancient enemies of sacred Israel;

Pilgrim and honorable native,

    were Hebrews of *this* Promised Land.

———

None were more stout and true

    than brave Hobomok,

An Indian friend from

    Wampanaug tribe,

    tall, bronzed and muscular

With eyes of a hawk,

    and sense of

    the forest about him.

Along with Squanto, Samoset, and tribe,

    Hobomok was a friend of Pilgrims,

    even the doubting Standish;

Hobomok admired a fair people of the Spirit,

    who were honest and kind,

Invincible in battle,

    and mighty in peace.

Nay, the Pilgrims were

    a sacred people

    of the forest;

Hobomok lived with them,

    keeping his wife and children,

    Safe from the savages

    whom they now pursued,

A threat to settler and native alike,

    including brave Hobomok,

Friend of the Pilgrim peoples,

    and native guide of the *Mayflower*.

Over the marching Pilgrims gleamed

the crimson banners of morning;

Beyond them, low on the distant horizon,

amidst the billowy clouds,

Was a battle-line of dark twilight

that, in regular order, retreated.

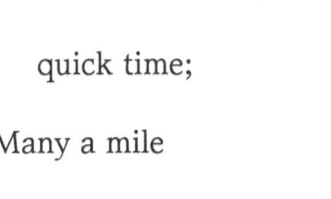

In the cool, early light,

the soldiers made

quick time;

Many a mile

they hurriedly marched

before the Pilgrim peoples

Woke from their sleep,

unaware of their militia's departure—

A tribe tended to its manifold labors,

and not to the quickening storm of battle.

Sweet was the air and soft;

Only a thin smoke from chimneys

Drifted over roofs of thatch,

and pointed steadily eastward.

Men came forth

from their doors,

and noticed the weather;

Said the wind had changed,

and blew well

for the *Mayflower*,

still resting in harbor.

Word soon spread of Standish's departure,

and all the dangers that menaced,

He being gone, the safety of the town,

and what to do in his absence.—

Many dark fears haunted

a people so alone in a forest.

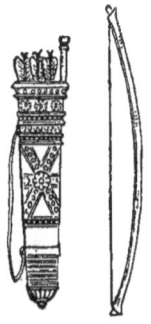

All though proceeded in Plymouth,

intent on its many

manifold labors;

Sufficient unto the day,

was the evil thereof,

All life's destiny unfolding,

God and People at work.

Merrily sang the birds,

    and the tender voices of women

Consecrating with hymns

    the common cares of household,

Making tidy nests of affection

    in the new-found, land of Zion.[14]

---

[14]Zion was the ancient name of Israel, the land promised by God to Moses and
his Hebrews. The Pilgrims often compared themselves to Hebrews.

Out of the sea rose the sun,

   and the clouds

   rejoiced at her coming;

Beautiful were her bright rays

   on purple tops of mountains;

Beautiful, too, on whited sails

   of the *Mayflower*

   resting in harbor,

Pure canvas on stout masts,

   able and ready for sea,

Once torn by winter's gales,

   but now mended by sailors' devotion.

Suddenly from the *Mayflower's* gunwale,

    darted a puff of smoke,

And floated seaward, effortlessly;

    Moments later was heard

Loud over field and forest

    the cannon's roar;

    Many echoes resounded

Repeating and reporting the sound;

    'Twas the signal-gun of departure!

"Alas," sighed the heart of the people,

    a sad farewell had come.

~Meekly, in voices subdued,

    were uttered prayers

    from the Bible,

Softly in the beginning,

    but ending in

    fervent appeals to God.~

All prayed for sailors homeward bound,

    and for settlers alone in Zion.

Then from their houses in haste

    came forth the Pilgrims of Plymouth,

Men, women and children,

    all hurrying

    down to the sea,

Anxious, with tearful eyes,

    to say farewell

    to the *Mayflower*,

Homeward bound over the ocean

    and leaving them here in the desert.

———

None were more anxious than John Alden;

    All night he had lain sleepless,

Tossing and turning with anguish,

    continuing to dwell on his troubles.

Alden had watched the mournful Standish,

coming back late from council,

Charging into the cottage dark,

muttering and murmuring to himself.

Sometimes the Captain prayed,

and sometimes he swore. ——

Once Standish strode toward Alden,

paused in a moment of silence,

But turned sharply away, saying:

"I will not awake him;

Let him sleep on, it is best;

what's the use of more talking?"

Then Standish darkened the lamp,

fell on his mattress,

Dressed as he was,

clothed for first light.

He cradled

pistol and saber

from brave battles past,

And fell asleep

as a soldier sleeps,

at the ready, expecting quick action.

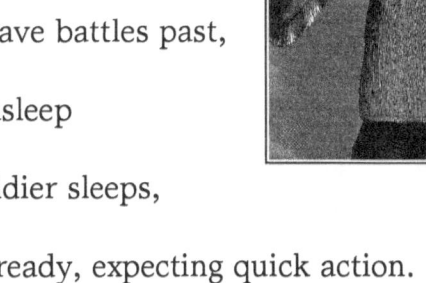

With the dawn, Standish arose,

   and, in the twilight, Alden beheld him.

The Captain wore breast-plate of steel,

   and the rest of knight's armor;

Buckled about his waist

   was his trusty blade

   of Damascus,

While in one hand,

   he grasped

   a sturdy musket,

   and strode quickly

   out of the chamber.

As he watched, John Alden

   ached and burned with regret.——

Trembling, he had wished to beg,

   seeking no less than pardon;

Thoughts of friendship beckoned,

   with their gentle and grateful emotions.

But a boy's hurt dimmed

his whispering angels —

Standish wrongly accused him of treason;

Alden still burned with the insult.

So Alden watched his friend

depart for war in anger;

Yet, Alden spoke not;

He watched Standish go forth to danger,

perhaps to death,

and yet spoke not!

Then Alden rose from his bed,

stepped into the light,

and heard what the people were saying;

Joined in the talk

of the town

with Stephen,

Richard and Gilbert,[15]

Joined in the

morning prayer

and in the reading of Scripture,

And, with Pilgrims all,

went hurrying down

to the sea-shore,

Down to Plymouth Rock,

the site of first landing,

Down to the great rock of the sea,

the corner-stone of a nation!

---

[15] Stephen Hopkins, Richard Gardiner, and Gilbert Winslow were fellow Pilgrims who arrived with the Mayflower in 1620.

There upon the beach

was the *Mayflower's* Master,

square-built and strong,

Just like the ship

he commanded,

with a nautical aroma about him.

The man spoke to this person and that,

while stuffing letters and parcels

Into his pockets capacious;

Alas, whispered messages mingled

Into a memory only so spacious,

till at last, he was wholly bewildered.

Near a small boat, Alden lingered,

  leaning to talk to the sailors,

One foot on the rowers' rail,

  And one foot firm on the rock.

The crew were eager for rowing,

  erect and prime on the benches,

 While Alden, too, was eager to go,

  and thus put an end to his anguish.——

He sought to flee from despair,

  faster than ship or canvas could sail,

Hoping to drown ghosts in the sea

    before they could rise and pursue him.

But as Alden glanced back at the shore,

    he beheld the form of Priscilla

Standing amidst the Pilgrims,

    observing all that was passing.

Fixed were her eyes upon his,

    as if she divined his intention,

Fixed with a look so sad,

    so reproachful, so imploring,

That with a sudden revulsion

    his heart recoiled

    from his purpose;

He stepped away from the cliff of the sea,

    where one more step was destruction.

Strange is the heart of man,

    with quick and mysterious instincts.

Strange is the life of man,

    with fated or fatal moments;

Fortune turns, as if on hinges,

    with sacred destiny unfolding.

"Here I remain!" Alden exclaimed,

    speaking to the heavens above.——

He thanked the Lord for dispelling

    the mist and the madness,

In which, blind and lost,

    a boy tempted death and destruction.

A mystical apparition then appeared,

   angelic wisps of mist and air,

   drifting silently over the horizon.——

"Behold," Alden whispered,

   "A snow-white phantom floats in the sky,

Like a hand that is pointing

   and beckoning over the ocean.

Yet, I feel another hand

   that is not so spectral and ghost-like,

Holding me back, drawing me here,

   and clasping mine for protection.

Float away, strange cloud,

    and vanish into the air!

Even if thy became as a fist,

    to threaten and awe me,

    I would not heed

Either your warning, menace,

    or omen of evil.

Priscilla I love dearly,

    even if my love cannot be;

There is no land so sacred,

    as the soil beneath her soft steps,

No air so pure or so pleasant,

    as the starry heavens above her.

Here in this land will I stay,

    and like an invisible presence

Hover around her forever,

    protecting and

    supporting her needs;

Yes! as my foot was the first

to step on this rock at this landing,

So, with the blessing of God,

shall it be the last at the leaving!"

Meanwhile alert was the *Mayflower's* Master,

a man of dignified air and importance,

Scanning with watchful eye

the aligning tide and weather;

A sailor is always impatient,

lest he lose the favoring current,

or the wind turn suddenly contrary.

The Master darted quickly to leave,

> and the people tarried along,

> Saying a few last words,

> and enforcing

> his careful remembrance.

Finally, the Master bid farewell,

> shook all hands, tipped his cap,

Clambered aboard with his men,

> and hastily rowed off to their vessel.

The Master was glad in his heart

> to be rid of much worry and flurry,

Glad to be gone from a land

> of sickness and sorrow,

A distant desert of empty shore

> and plenty of nothing but Gospel!

Lost in the sound of the oars

was the last farewell of the Pilgrims,

All strong hearts and true,

not one sailed back in the *Mayflower;*

Nay, not one looked back;

All had already

begun their calling,

As Christ, Son of God,

commanded,

keeping their hand

upon the plow,

and tilling

the land of the Lord.

Soon were heard on the *Mayflower*

    the shouts and grunts of sailors

Heaving and winding a chain,

    and hoisting their ponderous anchor.

Then the masts were braced

    and the sails filled;

    A mighty wind from the west,

Blew steady and strong,

    guiding the *Mayflower* from harbor.

She rounded the tip of Cape Gurnet,

and leaned far to the southward,

Passing islands and beaches of sand,

and the Field of First Encounter.

Taking the wind on her quarter,

she strove for the open Atlantic,

Borne on the height of the sea,

and the hopeful hearts of the Pilgrims.

Long in silence did the Pilgrims watch

the receding sail of the vessel,

Affectionately seen by all,

as something living and human.

———————

Then, as if touched by a spirit,

and rapt in vision prophetic,

One man removed his hat,

and bowed his head of whited hair.

This was the excellent

Elder of Plymouth,

William Brewster,

the Wise,

Saying, "Let us pray."

And they prayed,

and thanked the Lord

and took courage.

As they prayed, mournfully sobbed the waves

    bathing the rocks of the sea,

While above, upon the sainted land,

    winter wheat rustled in the wind,

Whispering across death's hill[16]

    where kindred spirits

Seemed to wake in their graves,

    and join in the prayer now uttered.

---

[16] Many Pilgrims died in the Winter of 1620-1621, then only a few weeks past. The victims were buried on a nearby hill.

Relentless and remorseless,

sailed away the *Mayflower*,

Onward to the rising sun,

on the eastern verge

of the ocean;

Her glowing sail slowly faded,

as if a quiet,

passing memorial,

Closing forever

all thoughts, all dreams

of ever returning to England.

The Pilgrims were lost in reflection

    when, lo! — in the shadowy distance

    they saw the form of an Indian,

Watching them from death's hill;

    Softly the people gestured and prayed,

Pointing with outstretched hands,

    and whispering, "Look!"

But it was too late;

    Friend or foe had already vanished.

All then walked silently home,

    but Alden lingered a little,

Musing and watching

    the surge of the ocean,

Ebbing and flowing,

    with a sparkle and shimmer of light,

Reflecting the spirit of God,

    moving visibly over the waters.

PRISCILLA

John Alden remains at the seashore, after other Pilgrims have returned to their homes. He watches the departing Mayflower *grow smaller and smaller upon the horizon.*

Alden glances down the beach. Broad expanses of virgin sand stretch to the horizon. Only the ocean's waves and the soft voices of seabirds can be heard.

After a while, Alden turns, and heads for home. To his surprise, he discovers he is not alone.

PRISCILLA

Thus for a while Alden stood,

    and mused by the shore of the ocean

Thinking of many things,

    and most of all, of Priscilla;

Then, as if thought had the power

    to draw to itself,

    whatsoever it conjures,

Whatsoever it touches,

    by the subtle laws of its nature,

There, as he turned to depart,

    Lo!—stood Priscilla behind him.

Alden froze in his steps,

    unable to speak, unable to move.

The Pilgrim maiden

    knew his discomfort,

    but she offered no solace, no quiet:

"Are you so offended by me,

    that you will not speak?" she asked.

"Am I so much to blame,

    that yesterday,

    when you were pleading

So warmly the heart of another,

    I pleaded for your own,

In an impulsive, wayward manner,

    perhaps forgetful of decorum?

Certainly you can forgive me

    for speaking so frankly;

I should not have said what I said,

    but now I can never unsay it;

For there are moments in life,

    when the heart is so full of emotion,

That, if by chance, it be disturbed,

by some fateful act or deed,

Or some careless word or thought,

it overflows its abundance,

Spilling forth its secrets,

never to be gathered again.

Yesterday I was disturbed,

when I heard you speak of Miles Standish,

Praising his warlike tendencies,

    changing his very defects into virtues,

Praising his courage and strength,

    and even his fighting in Flanders,

As if fighting alone

    could win the heart of a woman.

——

You do all men an injustice

    in exalting your hero.

Therefore I spoke as I did,

    by irresistible impulse.

You will forgive me, I hope,

    for the sake of our friendship,

Which is too true and too sacred

    to be broken this way!"

Thereupon answered Alden, the scholar,

friend of Standish, the warrior:

"I was not angry with you;

I was angry with myself,

Since I so badly

managed the matter."

"No!" interrupted the maiden,

with answer prompt and decisive;

"No; you were angry with me

for speaking so

frankly and freely.

This I know without doubt,

for it is the fate of a woman

Long to be patient and silent,

to wait like a ghost that is speechless,

Till some questioning voice

dissolves the spell of her silence.

This is the inner life

   of so many suffering women,

Sunless, silent, and hidden,

   like dark waters beneath the earth

Flowing through caverns of darkness,

   lost, unheard, and unseen,

Made weary by endless walls of stone,

   whispering eternal, profitless murmurs."

Thereupon answered boy Alden,

the would-be suitor of women:

"Heaven forbid it, Priscilla;

Women are not like depths unseen,

But more like beautiful rivers

that watered the Garden of Eden,

More like the river Euphrates,

nourishing the Biblical deserts of Havilah[17],

Making the land bloom in delight,

and memories sweet of the garden!"

---

[17] The "Biblical deserts" are in the Holy Land of the Middle East.

"Ah, by these words, I can see,"

    the maiden again interrupted,

"How very little you care

    for my thoughts and feelings.

Frankly and openly I spoke

    from the soul of my heart,

With pain and secret misgivings,

    hoping for sympathy and kindness;

Yet, straightway, you deflected my words,

    that are plain, direct, and in earnest,

Turning them from their meaning,

    and answering only with flattering phrases.

This is not right, this is not just;

This is not your true best;

For I know and esteem you,

a nature that is noble and fair,

Lifting me up to a higher,

more virtuous level.

Therefore I value your friendship,

and feel it more keenly

When you speak loosely,

for you value my feelings too little.

You utter those common

   and complimentary phrases

That thoughtless men think so fine,

   in dealing and speaking with women,

But which women reject as foolish,

   if not completely insulting."

Mute and amazed was Alden;

He listened and looked at Priscilla,

Thinking her never more fine or fair;

Divine was she in her beauty,

Speaking for womankind

With strength, clarity and truth,

Relating the injustices of men

and their foolish, simple airs.

Alas, empty was the youth

　　that was Alden the fledgling,

　　　　Who, but yesterday, glibly pleaded

　　　　　the cause of another;

　　　　He now struggled to plead his own,

　　　　　even as he longed to do so,

Fidgeting, embarrassed, and but silent,

　　vainly seeking an answer.

————

So the maiden continued to speak,

　　little divining or imagining

What was at work in his heart ——

　　affection, guilt, and regret.

"We shall be, as we are,"

　　promised the fair maiden,

　　"ever so faithful and loyal to truth,

Speaking what we think,

　　and honoring sacred friendship."

Then the maiden startled John Alden,

by revealing the secrets of her heart—

A boy's dream came true

but was now doomed by deeds so foolish.

"It is no secret I tell you," the maiden said,

"nor am I ashamed to declare it:

I have liked to be with you,

to see you, to speak with you always.

I was then hurt by your words,

 and your humbling bumble

Urging me to marry your friend,

 even if he be the great Captain Standish.

For I must tell you the truth:

 much more to me is your friendship

Than all the love he could give,

 were he twice the hero you think."

Then she extended her hand,

    and Alden gratefully grasped it;

Her soft touch healed his troubled heart,

    one aching and anguished so sorely.

    Suddenly the timid youth,

        found hidden courage:

    "Yes," said he, "forever

        shall we be friends,

        and of all people

    Let me be the truest,

        nearest and dearest!"

Then silence fell among them;

    All had been said, and both need ponder.

They cast a farewell look

    at the fading sail of the *Mayflower*,

Distant, but still in sight,

    a will-o'-the-wisp of the horizon.

Homeward together they walked,

with a strange, indefinite feeling,

As if all people had vanished,

leaving them alone in the desert.

But, as they strolled

through the fields

in the dancing light of morning,

Lighter grew their hearts, too,

and Priscilla said playfully:

"Now that our angry Captain is away,

doing battle in the forest,

Where he is happier by far

than leading a household,

You may speak frankly,

and tell me

all that happened

When you saw him last night,

and said how ungrateful you found me."

Thereupon answered John Alden,

    and told her the whole story, —

Told her of his own despair,

    and the dreadful wrath of Miles Standish.

Then the fair maiden smiled,

    and said between laughing and earnest,

"He is a little chimney,

    heated so hot in a moment!"

But Alden scolded her gently,

    reminding her of the Captain's burden,

    losing a wife and defending the people.

And, how he, John Alden, had likened

    to sail away in the Mayflower,

But had remained for her sake,

    on hearing the dangers that threatened, —

———

Suddenly her manner changed,

    and she said with

    a faltering voice,

"Truly I thank you

    for this,

    for caring

    for my manner

    and well-being."

Thus, Alden was truly

a Pilgrim devout,

journeying to Jerusalem,

hoping for wonders

of the Gospel,[18]

Taking three steps forward,

and one ever backwards,

Urged forward

by heavenly zeal,

but constrained by guilt and contrition.——

Slowly, but steadily onward,

receding yet ever advancing,

John Alden sought

a Holy Land of wonder,

but also a forbidden desire,

Urged on by the fervor of love,

but held back by an oath to a friend.

---

[18] In the Middle Ages, "pilgrims" were originally those who traveled to the Middle East to see the places visited by Christ.

THE MARCH OF MILES STANDISH

Captain Standish and his soldiers, along with their trusted Indian guide, Hobomok, continue their pursuit of hostile natives. The Pilgrim militia marches deeper and deeper into the thick, jungle-like forest.

The weather is cold and damp, trying their endurance. The soldiers wear heavy, steel armor, which chafes, causing painful sores.

Captain Standish is in a particularly foul mood. He mutters under his breath against his former friends, John Alden and Priscilla Mullins.

Thoughts of revenge, though, are a dangerous distraction upon the battlefield. No good can come from it.

THE MARCH OF MILES STANDISH

Stalwart Miles Standish

   marched steadily northward,

Struggling through forest and swamp,

   and along the trend of the sea-shore,

Day after day, with hardly a halt;

He strode steadily onward,

fueling a fever of war

That burned and crackled within;

Sulfur and gunpowder

Was more sweet to his liking

than all the scents of the forest.

Silent and moody the Captain marched,

and much repeated his anger——

He who had savored success,

and glorious victory in battle,

Was now flouted, rejected,

and scorned by a maiden,

And then betrayed and mocked

by a friend most trusted!

Ah! 'Twas too much to be borne——

An angry man chafed in his armor!

'I alone am to blame," the Captain muttered,

  "for mine was the folly.

What has a rough old soldier,

  grown grim and gray,

Tired by war and its ways,

  to do with the wooing of maidens?

'Twas but a dream,—let it pass,

  —let it vanish like so many others!

What I thought was a flower,

    was only a weed,

      and worthless;

Out of my heart will I pluck it,

    and henceforth

Embrace but terrible war and battle;

    Only danger shall I love!"

Thus repeated in his mind

   his sorry defeat and discomfort,

Whether he was marching by day

   or pondering at night in the forest,

Staring through the menacing branches,

   into the shadowy starlight beyond.

After three days' march

the Captain found an Indian encampment

Pitched on the edge of a meadow,

between the sea and the forest;

Women worked by their tents,

while warriors were painted for war,

Seated about a roaring fire,

smoking and talking together;

Lo, when the Indians saw

    the approach of the Captain's men,

Saw the menacing glint

    of armor, sword and musket,

Straightway the Indians were alert,

    and two of them stepped forth,

Rushing to parley with Standish;

    They offered furs as a present,

    and smiles for barter;

But friendship was only in their looks—

    Hatred was secretly in their hearts.

Warriors of the tribe were these,

    and brothers gigantic,

Huge as Goliath against David,

    or the terrible

King Og of Syria;

The name of one was Pecksuot,

    the other hailed

by Wattawamat.

Round their necks were suspended

    glistening knives

    in scabbards of shell,

Two-edged weapons for killing,

    with points as sharp as a needle.

No other weapons were flashed,

    except cunning, boast, and craft.

"Welcome, English!" said the braves[19],

    mimicking greetings from

Sailors on the seashore,

    but in a most sinister way.

Then in an Indian tongue

    they parleyed with Standish,

Speaking through

    the interpreter, Hobomok,

    the Pilgrim friend.

The braves asked for

    blankets and knives,

    but thirsted for muskets and gunpowder,——

Weapons of devils, the warriors mocked,

    along with deadly plague and pox,

Ready to be let loose,

    to scourge the Indian tribes!

---

[19]A "brave" is an Indian warrior.

But Standish refused to give guns,

    offering instead the Bible;

        Quickly did their tone change;

        The natives boasted

        and blustered

    As King Wattawamat advanced

    one stride after another,

And, with a lofty demeanor,

    swaggered to Pilgrim Standish:

"Now Wattawamat can see,

    by the fiery eyes

    of the Captain,

Angry is he in his heart;

    but the heart of the brave Wattawamat

Is not afraid at the sight;

    An Indian warrior is not by woman born,

But comes high on a mountain-top,

    from an oak-tree struck by lightning!"

Suddenly sprang forth Wattawamat,

    with all his weapons about him,

    Shouting, "Who is here to fight

        with brave Wattawamat?"

    Then he unsheathed his knife,

        wiped the blade on his hand,

    Held it aloft and displayed

        a woman's face on the handle;

He then said, with bitter expression

    and sinister meaning,

"I have another at home,

    with a man on the handle;

By and by they shall marry

    and bear plenty of children!"

Then stood forth Pecksuot, too,

    boastfully insulting Miles Standish;

This Indian too, patted a knife,

    that swung on his fiery neck;

He drew it half from its sheath,

and plunged it back firmly,

muttering as he did so:

"By and by, the light shall it see;

What it shall do, I shall say!

You, the mighty Captain

come in fear and trembling;

You want to conquer my braves

but it shall not be so.

You are a little man;

go and work with the women!"

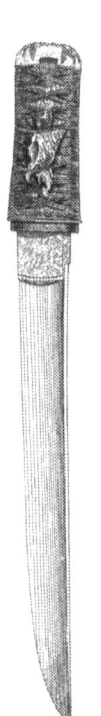

Meanwhile, Standish was alert

   to glimpses and shadows of Indians

Silently shifting and drifting

   from tree to tree in the forest,

Seemingly hunting for deer,

   eyes wide, arrows ready,

But encircling Standish's men,

   step by step in the hunt;

Quietly they drew closer,

   laying an ambush air-tight...

...But undaunted Standish stood,

   bluffing, dealing

   and unswerving,

As written in the old chronicles,

   praising the faith of our fathers.——

However, after the Indian defiance,

   the boast, the taunt, and the insult,

All the hot blood of Miles' race,

of Sir Hugh and

Thurston de Standish,

Boiled and burned in his heart,

throbbing the veins

of his temples.

Suddenly, headlong the Captain leapt,

snatching the Indian's knife,

raising it high overhead,

And plunging deep into the enemy;

Backward fell the stunned warrior,

His startled gaze locked upon the sky,

a horrid ferocity, frozen forever.

Straightaway arose from the forest,

the savage war-cry,

And, like the biting flurry

of a piercing, winter wind,

Came swift, sudden and keen

the flight of Indian arrows.

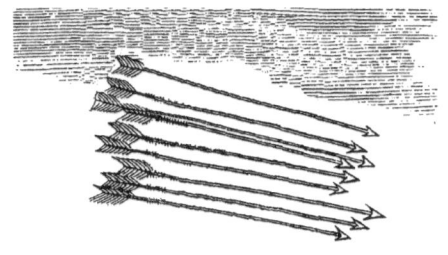

Then erupted the smoke of gunfire;

    Out of the burning cloud shot lightning,

From the lightning, echoed thunder;

    And death unseen ran before it.

Frightened the Indians fled

    for the nearby swamp and thicket,

Hotly pursued and afflicted;

    But their sachem[20], the fierce Wattawamat,

Fled not; he was dead.

    Cruelly and swiftly had a bullet

Passed through his head;

---

[20]A sachem is an Indian leader.

The warrior fell with both hands

clutching the grassy ground,

Stubbornly possessing in death,

the ancient land of his fathers.

———

In a moment all was silent,

the trumpet of death at rest.

There on the meadow plain,

the fallen warriors lay;

Standing above them,

Silent, with folded arms,

was Hobomok,

Indian friend of the Pilgrims.

Nodding and weary, he exclaimed

to the victorious Captain of Plymouth:

"Pecksuot bragged loudly,

of his courage, strength, and stature,—

Mocked did he, the great Captain,

and called him a little man;

but I see now

Big enough have you been

to lay him speechless before you."

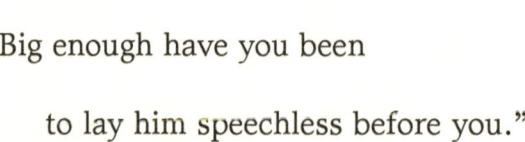

—Thus the first battle was won

by the hardy Captain Standish.

Soon the tidings thereof

drifted home to Plymouth,

Along with a ghastly

trophy of war,

the severe

head of the

fierce chief, Wattawamat,

Scowling from the roof

of the blackened hall,

that was both

a church and a fortress.

Some rejoiced at the horrific sight,

  and praised the Lord,

  for granting His courage;

Others protested and trembled;

  Hard were the wages

  of sin and vengeance —

  No good could come of it.

Only Priscilla averted

  her gaze from

  the gruesome trophy,

Thanking dear God

  in her heart that

  she had not married

  the hardy Standish,

Trembling, fearing, recoiling, lest,

  coming home from his battles,

The bloodied Captain should claim her hand,

  as a prize and reward for his valor!

THE SPINNING WHEEL

An interlude of quiet comes to Plymouth Colony. Spring turns to Summer and then Autumn of the year 1621.

The love-triangle remains unresolved. Captain Standish stays away, fighting other Indians, ever deeper into the forest.

John Alden and Priscilla Mullins remain friends, but no more. John Alden is still burdened by his promise to win the Pilgrim maiden for the absent Captain Standish.

One day, though, John and Priscilla make idle conversation, while Priscilla is doing household chores. A casual moment, though, unexpectedly becomes something else.

THE SPINNING WHEEL

The months of healing came,

    and in Autumn, the great ship, *Fortune*,

Arrived with family and friends,

    bringing cattle and grain for Pilgrims.

All rejoiced with tearful reunions

    and heartfelt embraces;

A nightmare of wintry death faded,—

    the dream of ages began.

The Pilgrim peoples went to work,

    settlers intent on their labors,

Hewing and hiving, thither and fro,

    raising gardens and stout fences —

They were sifting & plowing the soil,

    cutting the grass of the meadows,

Searching the sea for its fish,

    and hunting the deer in the forest.

All in the village was peace,——

    but yet, never far, drifted clouds of war,

Darkening the land with deadly alarm,

    filling stout hearts with fear and danger.

All fates rested on their absent militia,

    ten brave men on the march,

Led by their stalwart Captain Standish,

    scouring the menacing land with his forces.

A new Caesar was constantly gallant in battle

and defeating the alien armies;

A Roman incarnate struck fear and terror

among hostile Indian nations.

Yet, his troubled soul won not glory,

but the bitterness of hate's folly.

Anger was Standish's guide and idol,

filling him with guilt and contrition,

Which in all noble creatures,

follows the outbreak of passion.

The Captain's torment came like a sea tide rising,

enveloping the mouth of a river,

Pushing back its currents, clouding its waters,

and making it bitter and brackish.

The Captain suffered by day,

the outrages of forest and battle,

While at night he camped, apart,

eyed by his worried men and militia;

Brightly burned their Captain's anger

against friend and foe alike.

Yet, the Captain's face was also that of despair,

mixed with dreadful lament and regret.

Tired, tearful, and lonely was

the waning March of Miles Standish,

Anguished of soul, troubled in heart

and haunted by the dead.

Only of death and destruction,

    did word reach Plymouth,

Their stalwart Captain becoming

    as feared at home as abroad.

By nature's tide, Alden the fledgling

    ebbed from the Captain's shore,

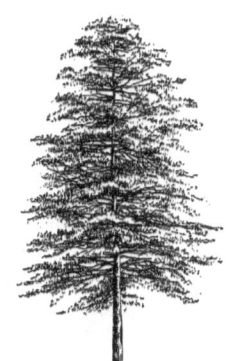

Disheartened and dismayed,

    and built a new abode

        in the woods,

Rough-hewn, solid and substantial,

    cut from firs of the forest.

Solid planked was

Alden's new home,

with a roof covered

with rushes;

Latticed his windows were,

but omitting glass

for thick paper,

Oiled to admit the light,

but excluding

wind and storm

of man and weather.

Like Matthew of the Bible,

   Alden dug a well,

   and around it

   planted an orchard,[21]

Sowing sweet vines of peace,

   and reaping God's fruit.

Still may be seen to this day

   some trace of the well and the orchard.

---

[21] Christ related a parable about a man who peacefully plants an orchard, but then confronts killers. *Matthew 21:33-41.*

Close to the house was the stall,

    where, safe, secure, and calm,

Was Raghorn, the snow-white steer,

    he being Alden's allotment

From the sharing of the cattle;

    The animal grazed nightly and sweetly

Over grassy pastures freshly mowed,

    and made fragrant with mint pennyroyal.

Often, when Alden finished his labors,

with eager feet

ran the dreamer

Along green, forest paths

leading to the

house of Priscilla,

Following illusions romantic,

& subtle deceptions of fancy,

Pleasure disguised as duty,

and love in the semblance of friendship.

Ever of her he thought,

    when he fashioned the walls of his dwelling;

Ever of her he thought,

    when he lovingly planted his garden;

Ever of her he thought,

    when he read

      the Bible on Sunday—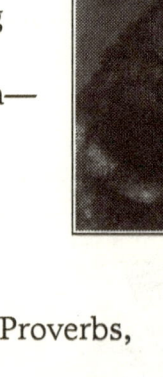

Verses warmly praising

    the virtuous woman—

How the heart of the

    husband doth trust

    the kind woman of Proverbs,

How all the days of his life,

    she will do him good, not evil,

How she seeketh the wool and the flax,

    and weave them with gladness,

How she layeth her hand to the spindle,

    and faithfully grace her calling,

How she fears not winter's chill,

    but admires the whited snow,

Since everyone is gently warmed

    by the scarlet felt of her weaving!

One afternoon in the Autumn

    Priscilla sat at a spinning-wheel,

Whirling, twirling, and twisting,

    making delicate yarn and thread.

John Alden sat with her idly,

    watching her dexterous fingers,

As if the thread she was spinning

    were his life and his fortune.

After a while and a moment,

he spoke to the murmur of the spindle:

"Truly, Priscilla," he said,

"when you are spinning and spinning,

Never an idle moment,

   but thrifty and thoughtful of others,

Suddenly you are transformed,

   and visibly changed in a moment;

You are no longer Priscilla,

   but Helena, an enchantress,

   and beauty of countless, mystical lands."

Like magic, the wonderful words

    cast a spell upon sensitive Priscilla;

Her light foot on the pedal

    became suddenly too swift;

    Her spinning wheel spun in a blur,

Uttered a protesting snarl,

    and broke its thread

    into many fine pieces.

Dreamy-eyed,

    the impetuous Alden,

    not heeding the

    mischief, continued:

"You are the

    beautiful Helena,

    the enchantress, the queen of a far-off land;

She whose story

    I heard as a child

    upon the streets of Old England,

Who, as she rode her gallant steed,

   over valley, meadow and mountain,

Enchanted her people with grace and quiet

   from a throne fixed to her saddle.

The queen was so thrifty and good,

   that her name passed into proverb.

So it shall be with your name,

   when the spinning-wheel fades

From our people's homes,

   ending their sweet, musical murmurs.

Then shall kindly mothers, intoning,

   recall the days of their childhood,

Praising magical moments of lore

   and the wonders of Priscilla,

   a swift and gracious spinner!"

Then the Pilgrim maiden smiled,

   stood and wound her delicate thread,

Pleased with the praise of her thrift

   from him whose praise was the sweetest.

She gathered from her table

    a snowy yarn of her spinning,

And made playful answer,

    to her suitor's flattery:

"Come, you must not be idle;

    If I am an idol for housewives,

Show yourself equally worthy

    of being the model for husbands.

Hold this yarn on your hands,

    While I wind it for the knitting;

Then who knows but hereafter,

    when all is long gone,

Children may hear kindly

    of John Alden, the winder!"

Thus, with a jest and a laugh,

    she wound the yarn

    on his hands,

He sitting awkwardly there,

    arms extended before him,

She standing graceful and tall

    winding the thread

    from his fingers,

Sometimes chiding and teasing

    his clumsy manner of holding,

Sometimes touching his hands,

    while she made tidy and smooth

The curling thread, unaware —

    for how could she know?—

That she sent heart-felt pulses

    into the very fabric of his soul.

———

Lo! in the midst of this scene,

    a breathless messenger arrived,

Bringing in hurry and haste

    terrible news from the village.

Miles Standish was dead!

— a friend said it was so,—

Slain by a poisoned arrow,

killed in front of the battle,

Into an ambush beguiled,

cut off with all his forces,

All the town would be burned,

and all the people be murdered!

———

Such were the tidings of evil

that burst on the hearts of the Pilgrims.

Silent and still,

Priscilla became

ashen and

anguished,

Eyes blankly staring,

numb and blind;

But stunned, too, was John Alden

   as if the tip of the same arrow

That pierced the heart of his friend

   had continued

   on to his own,

   sundering painfully

Once and forever,

   the bonds of duty,

   friendship, and regret.

———

 Surging too, was forbidden sensation,

   the quiet release of his freedom,

The end of his lingering guilt;

Unaware, Alden moved forward

Embracing, by instinct and nature,

   the motionless form of Priscilla,

Pressing her close to his heart,

   as forever his own, the love of his life.

For Priscilla,

all was as a dream,

a swirling vision

of hope and denial,

Of desires met and fulfilled,

mixed too,

with guilt and confusion —

The troublesome Captain

was no more,

but had she wished it so?

———

Yet, her love for Alden was true,

not a trace of destructive desire;

Both honored the Captain in his absence,

staying respectfully apart,

And now both felt keenly

    the pain of his death,

    a soldier who died for them,

Gallant to the end,

    struggling in an unsung cause,

A new world yet to be born,

    a Pilgrim's heaven,

    a journey to the stars.

———

Such are distant beads of rain,

    from lonely & separate sources,

Each seeing the other from afar,

    falling amidst the pebbles,

    and quietly streaming.

Each has its own winding path,

    but yet draw nearer and nearer,

Rushing together at last,

    at their gathering place in the forest;

So these lives had once been,

    moving in distant, and separate streams,

Coming in sight of each other,

    then diverting and flowing asunder,

Parted by barriers strong,

    but yet drawing nearer and nearer,

Rushing together at last,

    until each was lost in the other.

THE WEDDING DAY

With the death of Miles Standish, John Alden is released from his promise to win Priscilla for his former friend. The young Alden proposes marriage, and Priscilla accepts.

Fate comes full circle. The original messenger, John Alden, inherits the message, i.e. win the hand of the beautiful maiden.

The surviving Mayflower Pilgrims gather for the wedding of John and Priscilla. Their religious elder, William Brewster, along with William Bradford, the Governor of the colony, preside over the ceremony.

A surprise, though, awaits everyone.

THE WEDDING DAY

Forth from the curtain of clouds,

    a shroud of purple and scarlet,

Rose the sun, the great High Priestess,

    in garments resplendent,

Holiness unto the Lord,

    written in dazzling rays of light,

While round the hem of her robe

    lay golden fields and fruits of glory.

This was the wedding day

of Priscilla, the Pilgrim maiden.

Friends gathered together

with Governor Bradford and Elder Brewster,

Gracing the sacred moment

with the Law and the Gospel,

One with the sanction of earth

and one with the blessing of Heaven.

Simple and brief

was the wedding,

like that of

Ruth and Boaz,

forebears of

King David and Christ.

Softly the youth

and the maiden

repeated the

words of betrothal,

Receiving each other

for husband and wife

in witness of all the people;

This was the Pilgrim way,

and the honorable

custom of Holland,

kind host of Pilgrims in olden days[22].

---

[22] The Pilgrims lived in Holland for a decade in the early 1600's.

Fervently then, and devoutly so,

the excellent Elder of Plymouth

Warmly prayed for home and hearth,

Asking for grace and loving affection,

A life of sacrifice and selfless devotion

and imploring divine benediction.

All though, was not as expected,

the grand day not yet concluded;

Lo! When the service was ended,

a form suddenly appeared,

beyond the Church entry,

Clad in rusting armor and steel,

and slumped so sadly and so heavily!

All were aghast and perturbed

by the sudden, uninvited arrival.

Lo! Why does the groom startle and stare

at the strange apparition?

Lo! Why does the bride turn pale,

and clutch to her husband so?

Lo! What could be so upsetting?

 Was it of this world or the next?

Was it a phantom of air,

 —a bodiless, ghostly illusion?

Was it a soul from the grave,

 risen to forbid

 and to haunt the living? —

Long had it stood there unseen,

 a guest mysterious

 and unwelcomed.

Its eyes were clouded and gray,

 but held a most remarkable expression,

Softening a dire gloom

 and revealing a warm glow;

His gaze was like a somber sky

 filled with clouds of storm,

But parting for a moment,

 and showing the sun by its brightness.

Then the ghost lifted its hand,

and moved its lips, —

Yet, only silence was heard,

As if an unseen spirit

had quieted a fleeting intention.

But then ended the wedding,

the prayer,

and the last benediction;

Into the room

strode the apparition

shedding its

mysterious illusion.

Bodily there,

clad in his armor

was Standish,

the Captain of Plymouth!

Stepping forth, arm outstretched,

the soldier greeted Alden the fledgling,

Shaking the bridegroom's hand,

and conversing quickly with emotion:

"Forgive me! I have been angry and hurt,

—too long have I clutched this feeling;

Cruel and hard have I been,

but now it is over,

Thank God!

Many pardons I beg,

for my passions surged—

Mine is the hot blood

that flowed in the veins of Hugh Standish,

Sensitive and swift to resent,

but now swift in atoning for error.

Never so much as now

was Miles Standish

the friend of John Alden."

Thereupon answered the bridegroom:

"Let the past be quickly forgotten,—

Except for dear, old friendship,

graceful in age and memory,

never passing, forever young."

Then the Captain advanced,

   bowed, and saluted Priscilla,

With all the grace and humility

   of the classical gentry of England,

A refined air of soldier and noble,

   town and country as one,

Wishing her a joyful wedding,

   and freely praising her husband.

Then smiling so wryly, the Captain added:

"I should have remembered the adage,—

If you would be well served,

you must do it yourself;

and moreover,

No man gathers flowers abroad

when they belong to another!"

———

Great was the people's amazement,

and yet greater their rejoicing,

Thus to behold once more

the sun-burnt face of their Captain.

They sadly mourned him in death,

but gladly raised him to life,

Eager to know and to hear his wonderful tale,

quickly forgetting bride and bridegroom.

The Pilgrims prodded and regaled their hero,

    each interrupting the other,

Till the good Captain declared,

    being quite overpowered

    and bewildered,

He'd rather charge

    an Indian encampment,

Than, ever again,

    be at a wedding

    to which he had not

    been invited!

Meanwhile the bridegroom quietly withdrew

    and took leave with his bride,

Stepping into the bright sun and clear air

    of that crisp and beautiful morning,

A vision complex and mysterious,

    of glory and dusk compounded.

 Blessing the world

the sun had come that day,

revealing vapory airs beneath her,

A heavenly mist drifting softly

across a shimmering, blue sea.

Yet, the colors of Autumn

were also muted and quiet,

casting a light lonely and sad.

Visible too clearly on Burial Hill

were somber memorials

of loss and privation——

Brightly lit were the graves of the dead,

asleep with the whispers of the sea.

There too, was

the new-found land,

of forest, meadow,

and shore,

Hope mingled with loss,

nature's bounty

yet to be measured.

To the knowing eyes of

John and Priscilla,

all could still be as

the Garden of Eden,

Blessed with

the promise of God,

whose voice was the

whisper of the sea.

Soon their thoughts were disturbed,

    by the noise and stir of departure,

Friends coming forth from chapel,

    and impatient of

    longer delaying,

Each with a plan

    for the day,

    work not to be

    left for the morrow.

Then, in a commotion,

    from a simple corral,

    came exclamations

    of wonder,

Alden, the thoughtful and the careful,

    being so happy and proud of Priscilla,

Reserved one last surprise,

    one final touch for the wedding day.

Fetching gently his snow-white steer,

who sweetly obeyed the hand of its master,

Alden haltered its stout neck

and guided it to the head of the procession;

He draped a scarlet cloth on its hind,

and fixed a pillow for a saddle.——

"A bride walks not," he said,

"through the dust

and the heat of the day;

Nay, she should ride like a queen,

not plod as a humble peasant."

Priscilla was reluctant at first,

but reassured

by guests and Elder,

Pressed softly on the cushion,

grasped the hand

of her husband,

And gaily, with joyous laughter,

A princess mounted her noble steed.

"Nothing is missing now,"

said Alden with a smile,

"but the throne of the land;

Then you would be in truth

my queen,

my beautiful Helena!"

Onward the bridal procession

now moved to a new habitation

For happy husband and wife,

their friends following closely together.

They crossed the watery ford in the forest,

a glittering, murmuring stream,

Pleased with the couple that passed,

softly reflecting lovers in a dream—

Graceful, floating in air,

the beauty of this world and beyond.

Down through the bright, autumn leaves

 the sun was pouring her splendors,

Glittering on dew-misted grapes,

upon mingling vines suspended,

Releasing their sweet aroma

into the freshness of the forest,

Wild and lush as the sacred garden

of the Valley of Eshcol,

as promised by God to ancient Israel.

Like a picture it seemed

    of by-gone, angelic ages,

Fresh with the youth

    of the world, recalling

    Rebecca & Isaac,

    son of Abraham,

    father of three faiths.[23]

———

Thus was the courtship

    & wedding of Pilgrim lovers,

Old and yet ever new,

    simple & beautiful always,

Love immortal and young

    in the endless

    succession of lovers.

---

[23]Abraham is a revered prophet of Judaism, Christianity, and Islam.

*So through the magical forest
passed onward the bridal procession...*

EPILOGUE

The romantic adventures of Priscilla, John, and Captain Standish come to a pleasant close. All are dear friends again.

Good tidings await. Priscilla and John have many children. The Captain meets a certain young woman, named Barbara, recently arrived on the supply ship, Fortune.

Their many descendants include a leader of the American Revolution, John Adams, and his son, John Quincy Adams. Both become Presidents of a new nation – the United States of America.

Moreover, family members tell and retell the tale of the Pilgrim lovers. Their story passes from generation to generation, until it is set to verse by a great-grandson. His name is Henry Longfellow, a great American poet.

All, indeed, can live happily ever after.

The End

Selected Bibliography

The Romance of Pilgrims is based on historic sources, including government and university archives. This bibliographical essay summarizes the main sources, but is by no means exhaustive.

The Text – *The Romance of Pilgrims* is adapted from Henry Longfellow's *The Courtship of Miles Standish* of 1858 (Boston: Ticknor, Fields, 1858), but also loosely follows the theatrical format of a later 1903 edition (Indianapolis: Bobbs-Merrill, 1903).

Primary Illustrations – Longfellow's first edition of 1858 had no illustrations, but his *Courtship* edition of 1876 (Boston: James R. Osgood and Company, 1876) contained miniature, jewel-like engravings. These images were digitally restored for this revival, e. g. John Alden's lonely walk in the forest, and the final wedding procession.

An 1888 edition of *The Courtship of Miles Standish* (Boston: Houghton, Mifflin, 1888) had highly-stylized engravings by the renown F.T. Merrill, George H. Boughton, C.S. Rheinhart, and Granville Perkins. Scenes included Captain Standish pacing in his cottage, and Priscilla and John at the spinning wheel. [The author warmly thanks the Special Collections Department of the University of California at Davis for providing scans of engravings from the 1888 edition of *The Courtship of Miles Standish,* as well as images from W.H. Bartlett's *The Pilgrim Fathers* (London: A. Hall, Virtue & Company, 1853).]

The 1903 edition of *The Courtship of Miles Standish* (Indianapolis: Bobbs-Merrill, 1903) printed innovative illustrations in color, based on the work of Howard Chandler Christy. Some of the images appear in this book as full-page, high-contrast, black-&-white engravings, e.g. Standish's battle with the Indians. Mr. Christy also sketched the finely-shaded vignettes that open each chapter.

In addition, the artist, A.S. Burbank, painted an independent version of the Pilgrim lovers in 1904. His work appeared in A. C. Addison's *The Romantic Story of the Mayflower Pilgrims* (Boston: L.C. Page & Company, 1911), and is reproduced in the introduction of this book.

Reproductions of paintings by Rembrandt and the "Dutch Masters," were originally published in Europe around the time of the First World War. Many are reprinted here for the first time in several generations.

The German publisher, Deutsche Verlags-Anstalt of Stuttgart, issued the monumental collections, *Rembrandt,* by Adolf Rosenberg in 1909; *Fran Hals* by W.R. Valentiner in 1921; and *Van Dyck* by Emile Schaeffer in 1909. The Studio of London, England produced *The Great Painter-Etchers, from Rembrandt to Whistler* by Malcolm C. Salaman in

1914; and a *Treatise on Landscape Painting in Water Colors* by David Cox in 1922. William Heineman of London printed *Great Masters of Landscape Painting* by Émile Michel in 1910.

Supplemental Illustrations – Most images of the Roman Empire are from the biography, *Julius Caesar* by W. Warde Fowler (New York: G.P. Putnam's Sons, 1895); and Charles Boutell's *Arms and Armor in Antiquity and the Middle Ages* (New York: Charles Scribner, 1871).

Engravings of colonial settlers, natives, and soldiers are from *A Popular History of the United States* by William Cullen Bryant and Howard Sidney Gay (New York: Charles Scribner's Sons, 1878). Additional images are from *My Friend, The Indian* by James McGlaughin (Boston: Houghton-Mifflin, 1910) and *The History of North America, Volume II: The Indians of North America in Historic Times* by Cyrus Thomas (Philadelphia & London: George Barrie & Sons, 1903).

Louis Rhead's illustrated version of *The Pilgrim's Progress* (New York: The Century Company, 1898, 1912, 1916) supplied images of a Pilgrim in anguish, which appear as John Alden's panic at the beach. The Library of Congress offers more traditional views of the Pilgrims landing at Plymouth Rock, including an engraving by Currier & Ives for the American Centennial of 1876. For the Bicentennial of 1976, the U.S. Government Printing Office similarly included Pilgrims and Indians in *Art in the United States Capitol* (Washington, DC: GPO, 1976).

Historic printer's ornaments are from Dover Publications and Hart Publishing. *The Illustrators Handbook, The Great Giant Swipe File* (New York: Hart Publishing, 1978) offers an extensive collection of historic engravings on virtually any topic, while *A Compendium of Frames and Borders in the Public Domain* (New York: Hart Publishing, 1983) provides medieval and Victorian decorations.

A very rich source is the Dover Pictorial Archive, a series of professional design books by Dover Publications of Mineola, New York. *Early American Design Motifs* (Dover, 1974) by Suzanne Chapman reproduces the lively bird and floral decorations of Colonial America; *Curious Woodcuts of Fanciful and Real Beasts: A Selection of 190 Sixteenth-Century Woodcuts ...{by} Konrad Gesner* (Dover, 1971) includes an unforgettable visage of a scowling, medieval cat. Fine supporting images come from Jim Harter's *Men, A Pictorial Archive from Nineteenth-Century Sources* (Dover, 1980) and *Animals: 1419 Copyright-free Illustrations of Mammals, Birds, Fish, Insects, etc.* (Dover, 1979); *Traditional Floral Designs and Motifs* by Madeline Orban-Szontagh (Dover, 1989); and *Treasury of Bible Illustrations* by Julius Schnorr von Carolsfeld (Dover, 1999).

About the Authors

Henry Longfellow was America's most popular poet of the nineteenth-century. He is still renown for his legendary, historical ballads, including *Song of Hiawatha; Evangeline; and Paul Revere's Ride.* His love-story, *The Courtship of Miles Standish*, was a runaway bestseller for decades, continuing well into the early twentieth-century.

In his later years, Henry Longfellow was a professor at Harvard University; he died in 1882. His elegant, colonial-era home is now a popular historic site in Cambridge, Massachusetts.

David W. Bradford has graduate degrees from Harvard and Yale Universities. He has studied the Mayflower Pilgrims for more than two decades; this book is part of a planned series about the colonial settlers of America.

Mr. Bradford also writes about religion and current events. The author is represented by the East-West Literary Agency, whose clients include NBC television. Mr. Bradford divides his time between the East and West Coasts, doing research for his books.